LIFE WITH DEREK

BREAKUP BLUES

A novelization by Heather Alexander

Based on the teleplays from the TV series created by Daphne Ballon

Grosset & Dunlap

GROSSET & DUNLAP
Published by the Penguin Group
Penguin Group (USA) Inc., 375 Hudson Street, New York, New York 10014, USA
Penguin Group (Canada), 90 Eglinton Avenue East, Suite 700, Toronto, Ontario M4P 2Y3, Canada
(a division of Pearson Penguin Canada Inc.)
Penguin Books Ltd., 80 Strand, London WC2R 0RL, England
Penguin Group Ireland, 25 St. Stephen's Green, Dublin 2, Ireland
(a division of Penguin Books Ltd.)
Penguin Group (Australia), 250 Camberwell Road, Camberwell, Victoria 3124, Australia
(a division of Pearson Australia Group Pty. Ltd.)
Penguin Books India Pvt. Ltd., 11 Community Centre, Panchsheel Park, New Delhi—110 017, India
Penguin Group (NZ), 67 Apollo Drive, Rosedale, North Shore 0632, New Zealand
(a division of Pearson New Zealand Ltd.)
Penguin Books (South Africa) (Pty.) Ltd., 24 Sturdee Avenue,
Rosebank, Johannesburg 2196, South Africa

Penguin Books Ltd., Registered Offices:
80 Strand, London WC2R 0RL, England

Cover photo by Stephen Scott, Courtesy of Shaftesbury Films Inc.

Library of Congress Cataloging-in-Publication Data is available.

ISBN 978-0-448-44909-8   10 9 8 7 6 5 4 3 2 1

CHAPTER ONE

Dear Diary,

I can't stop smiling.

Seriously. I've suddenly become that weird fifteen-year-old who smiles all the time. Unheard of. I don't think I've ever been this super-happy. Well, okay, maybe when I got that double A+ on the English exam and everyone else pretty much bombed it. But this happiness is way different. Max makes me smile. All the time.

It's been two weeks, five days, and thirteen hours since we started going out. I know, because I can't stop thinking about him. How cute he is. How he hates tomatoes on sandwiches. How his hand is warm but not sweaty when he holds mine. We met at a party that Kendra, Derek's girlfriend, threw to find me a guy. Totally lame idea, that's true. All the guys she rounded up for me were losers. I'd gone into a bedroom to hide, sure I'd die single and alone (it all seemed

3

kind of tragic)—and in walked Max. He said he was looking for the bathroom. But if you believe in fate, like I do, you have to know—on some level—he was really looking for me. Nature was calling to him—just not in the way he originally thought.

So I'm up and dressed with nothing to do but write, and I still have thirty minutes before I have to go to school. Max does that to me. I'm going to hang out by his locker so I can see him before first period. Wait—George, my stepfather, is going on a business trip today, so that means he can't drive me on his way to work. If Mom drives me to school, I'll never get there on time. By the time she drops Marti at the elementary school, and Lizzie and Edwin at the middle school, I'll be lucky to make it to the high school before the bell rings. Mom used to be so much more organized before George and his three kids came into our lives. Everything ran smoothly at the McDonald house when it was just Mom, me, and Lizzie—then Mom fell in love and married George Venturi. She says George and his kids add fun into our lives. Depends on your definition of fun. Edwin is fun and little Marti is definitely funny. But then there's Derek. A self-centered stepbrother exactly my age who goes to the same school = NOT fun.

Whoa. I'm not going to rant about Derek today. Nothing—not even Derek—can ruin my good mood.

Hey . . . maybe Derek can give me a ride to school.

In your dreams, Casey!

Or maybe I can text Max and ask him to pick me up. I mean, we are a couple now. Couples do everything together. They share thoughts and dreams and frozen mochaccinos. There are no secrets if you're a perfect couple—like Max and me. Now that I think of it, I know Max's favorite color (green) and his favorite food (bacon cheeseburger) but I don't know his favorite animal or his feelings on global warming. We need to share more . . . we need to tell each other absolutely everything!

Really? So you're gonna tell Max that you still sleep with Bobo, the stuffed rabbit? And he gets to know that you sing Britney Spears songs in the shower? Brave girl.

♡ Love,

Casey

• • • • •

"Derek. Derek? Are you listening to me?" Kendra demanded.

"Uh . . . sure," Derek replied. He gave her hand a small squeeze as they walked down the crowded hall together.

"So don't you think that Natalie was wrong? She *never* should have said that to Jenna." Kendra flipped her long blond hair out of her eyes and stopped abruptly. "Don't you agree?"

Derek tried to rewind the conversation in his mind. *What is Kendra talking about?* He didn't have a clue. "About what?"

"Derek!" Kendra squealed. She playfully slapped his arm. "You weren't listening to me at all!"

"Sorry." Derek smiled sheepishly at his beautiful girlfriend. She looked good today in that blue fuzzy sweater. He liked the way it matched her eyes.

"So what were you thinking about?" Kendra asked. She reached up and tucked a piece of Derek's messy, light brown hair behind his ear.

Derek ran his fingers through his hair, rumpling it up again. She was always doing that. "Thinking about when?"

"Before, when I was talking to you about Natalie and Jenna's fight."

Derek tried to remember. It seemed so long ago. Burritos. That was it. He was thinking about eating a burrito. He liked burritos. "Nothing," he said.

"Oh, Dere-bear," Kendra cooed. "You need to pay attention more." She slipped her arm through his as they continued down the hall.

"Hi, Kendra!" several girls called out. Kendra smiled

at them. She was mega-popular and she knew it. Together with Derek, they were the "it" couple of Sir John Sparrow Thompson High School. Everyone agreed that with their hot, movie-star looks they were meant for each other. Some kids had even started calling them "Kend-rek." It made Derek want to barf, but he never told Kendra. She seemed to love it.

"Derek, my man!" Sam and Ralph greeted Derek.

"Hey!" Derek was glad to see his friends.

"Where were you yesterday?" Sam demanded. "We really needed your Dere-dunk. We were crushed by those guys from Central."

"Crushed? No way! We need a rematch," Derek cried. Kendra had dragged him to some lame chick flick, and he had missed their pickup basketball game in the park.

"Done," said Ralph. "Today at four. You in?"

"I'm all over 'em." Derek dribbled an imaginary ball.

"Dere-bear." Kendra's hand blocked his imaginary slam-dunk. "I thought we might study together after school."

Derek watched his two friends snicker. *This is not me,* he thought. *This is not the guy I am.* He needed to show that he was in control. "Kendra, I'm playing ball with my guys. Important game, you know. We'll hang after."

7

Derek could see Kendra start to pout. He hated the pout.

"But, Dere—"

Luckily, the bell rang. Kids started sprinting to class.

"Gotta run." Derek kissed Kendra on the cheek and took off for the open door across the hall. He couldn't believe he was racing for the safety of math class.

He slumped into his seat. The teacher began to write equations on the board. He pulled his math book out of his bag and flipped it open. A little lavender slip of paper fluttered to the ground.

"Love note?" whispered Ralph, who sat across from Derek. Ralph snickered and leaned down to reach for it.

Derek quickly snatched the piece of paper. He knew it was from Kendra even before he looked at it. She was always leaving him notes—in his books, in his locker, in his wrestling bag. He had no idea when she slipped them in. When they first started dating three months ago, he thought it was really sweet. Now it was kinda annoying.

"See you at lunch, Dere-bear. Can't wait to tell you about dress shopping with princess Tara!

Kisses, K."

Derek crumpled the note and shoved it in his pocket.

Tara was Kendra's cousin who was getting married. Kendra thought Tara was totally spoiled—or some such family thing. All Derek knew was that lately Kendra was always complaining about her. Whatever. He had two new stepsisters to bother him. He couldn't handle being bothered by Kendra's family, too.

When math class and English class ended, Derek met Sam and Ralph in the bathroom. He dumped his books on the slimy tiled floor and hoisted himself onto the windowsill and leaned back. He had no fear of falling out of the second-floor window. The window was so warped and had been painted shut years ago. It was where he went to chill with his guys. Sam and Ralph gave him a play-by-play of the basketball massacre. Derek couldn't believe their team had folded so easily.

"And then," Sam recounted, "Ralph completely flubbed the foul shot—"

"It wasn't my fault!" Ralph cried. "There was this massive sun glare—"

Derek's phone buzzed. He pulled it from his pocket and glanced at the text message.

"And, what, you went all Helen Keller and couldn't toss the ball in?" Derek teased.

"If you had been there," Ralph replied, "you would've

known that that was not the way it was." Derek's phone buzzed again. He gazed down. Another text.

"Who's texting you?" Sam asked.

"No one," Derek replied. "Who else is playing this afternoon?" Another buzz.

Ralph laughed. "Girlfriend, right?"

Derek nodded. He knew if he didn't answer, Kendra wouldn't stop. Couldn't a guy find some peace in the bathroom?

WHERE R U? W8TING @ LUNCH. HURRY! XOXOX K.

"Time for lunch, guys," Derek said.

"She totally controls you," Ralph said.

"No, she doesn't. I'm just hungry," Derek insisted. "Really hungry."

• • • • •

"Why aren't you eating your french fries?" Kendra asked. She kept her hand rested on his knee, while she reached over and grabbed a couple of fries.

"Not hungry, I guess," Derek muttered.

"That's weird for you," Kendra said. "What's wrong?"

"Nothing." Derek eyed his friends at the end of the table. They were kicking back, headphones on, inhaling their sloppy joe specials. He felt suffocated between Kendra and her girlfriend Natalie.

"So, Dere, I was telling Nat that you totally think it was Jenna's fault, right?"

Derek nodded. *Is it just Kendra or does every girlfriend act this way?* he wondered. He scanned the cafeteria. Casey and Max sat two tables away. Casey was scribbling furiously in a mini-notebook. Derek couldn't hear above the noise, but it looked like she was interviewing Max. Weird, but that was Casey. Max was smiling, but his smile seemed a little dazed. Derek sighed. Max was about to be turned into the living dead, too.

Derek turned back to Kendra. He watched her lick ketchup off her glossy lips. She was really so pretty.

"Derry," Kendra whispered in his ear as they all left the cafeteria. "I really wanted to be alone with you for a little while today. Just you and me."

"But I promised the guys I'd shoot some hoops."

"I know. Just meet me on the bleachers after school. You can go to your game after some you-and-me time." Kendra stood on her tiptoes and gave him a hug. Derek smiled. Maybe he'd been too harsh. She was his girlfriend after all.

After school, Derek hurried to the bleachers. *Kissing*

on the bleachers—that's what this boyfriend-girlfriend thing is about, he thought. Kendra was already there.

"Hey, you." Derek wrapped his arms around her. She always smelled so good. Kind of like vanilla and flowers.

"Hey." She gave him a quick kiss. Derek leaned in for another, but Kendra pulled back. She opened her pink plaid messenger bag and grabbed a bunch of pages torn from a magazine.

"I need to know what you think," she said.

"I think you smell nice." Derek kissed her cheek. Her skin was soft.

Kendra pushed him away. "Dere! Seriously, I have to meet Tara tonight. What do you think about these dresses? Do you think I should do sleeveless or not? Is a one-shouldered dress too much for a bridesmaid?"

Derek's head was spinning. What was she talking about? "I don't know," he admitted. "Why are you asking me?"

"Because you're my boyfriend, silly. Come on, pick a dress!" She thrust the clippings at him. "Remember I want to wear the shimmery petal pink polish on my fingers and toes, so I don't want the dress to be too sparkly."

"Why don't *we* kiss and *you* talk about this with Tara or Natalie?" Derek wrapped his arms around her again.

"Because you are my boyfriend. We should do everything together."

Derek stood. "Look, Kendra, I don't really care what dress you wear. Really."

Kendra's face crumpled as if she'd been slapped. She bit her lip and stared down at the pictures in her lap. "Oh, if that's the way you feel . . ."

Derek sighed. He hated making her sad. Why was this relationship thing so complicated? *If only she could take a step back, get out of my face a bit,* he thought. But he didn't know how to tell her.

He sat down. "Hand over those pictures," he said, forcing his best boyfriend-who-cares smile. "Let's play *Project Runway.*"

CHAPTER TWO

"Hey, Casey."

Casey looked up. She loved the way Max said her name. He leaned against the locker next to hers.

"Hi," she said. She reached into her locker and grabbed the first two books her hand touched. Usually at the end of every day, Casey carefully ran through the homework checklist she wrote in her assignment pad. She made extra sure she had the correct books for the night. Right now, with Max's bright blue eyes smiling at her, *any* book was fine.

"What are you up to?" he asked.

"Up to?"

"Yeah." Max gave her a strange look. "Like what are you doing after school?"

"Going home?" Casey hoped that was the right answer. She was new to this whole boyfriend-girlfriend thing.

Maybe there was a better answer. She always liked to get answers right.

"Wanna ride?"

"With you? In your car?" Casey could suddenly hear how silly she sounded. Cute, popular Max sometimes made her nervous.

"Yeah. Come on." Max smiled. He shut her locker and grabbed her book bag.

I'm going home in my cute boyfriend's cool car! Casey wanted to yell to all the kids in the hallway. Especially the really popular girls. It took a lot of willpower to keep quiet. Max had been born into the popular crowd. But Casey knew she had to tread lightly. With Max, she'd suddenly been included, too—but it was like having a visitor's visa. Without Max, she could face social deportation at any time.

"Dude!" Max's friend Clink called.

"Later," Max called. He reached for Casey's hand and pulled her close. Casey smiled up at him. She loved that he wasn't embarrassed to hold her hand in front of his friends.

"You are so lame," Clink taunted.

Max chuckled and ignored his friend, giving Casey's hand a little squeeze.

"Why'd he say that?" Casey whispered to Max. Did Clink think *she* was lame?

"Just a guy thing," Max said. "No biggie."

"But—" Before Casey had a chance to pull apart the quick conversation and analyze it, like she liked to do, she spotted Emily waving. Emily stood with Sheldon Shlepper outside the main school doors. Casey knew that lots of kids thought super-popular Max and teacher's pet Casey were a weird couple. Hey, she still had trouble believing it herself! But her hip, best friend Emily and nerdy, whiny Shlepper were *the* most confusing duo ever. Casey couldn't wrap her mind around that relationship. But she had decided that if Shlepper rocked Em's world, then that was cool with her.

"Where are you two off to?" Emily asked. She wiggled her eyebrows.

Casey blushed. "Max is driving me home." She pointed to his hot red car in the parking lot. Not that she had to. Everyone knew Max's car.

"Sweet ride," Shlepper said. Casey knew that Shlepper was car-less. Poor guy. He still took the bus home. Okay, up until a few minutes ago *she* still took the bus home. But that was totally different.

"Wanna lift?" Max offered.

Casey squealed. "Really?" She bounced on her toes. "That's great. Come on, Em! You guys'll go in the back seat." This was so cool. It was like a double date. How very couple-like!

Emily and Shlepper squeezed in and Casey settled into the front seat. She couldn't help grinning as she clicked her seat belt into place. She felt so important. Like royalty. Sitting up front with her boyfriend as they drove another couple home. Casey opened the window and let the breeze blow her long brown hair as they drove.

"What are you guys up to this weekend?" Emily asked.

"Football," Max said.

"Have you seen Max play?" Casey turned around in her seat. "He's amazing! Do you know he's scored seven touchdowns and the season isn't half over?"

"That's great," Emily said.

"He's the fastest runner on the team. He, like, flies. He's definitely the best player we have," Casey bragged. "He should be first string running back all the time. I don't know why the coach put you on second string last week."

Max shook his head. "We have lots of great players. Everyone gets a chance."

"Oh, come on. You're so the best." Casey debated

writing an editorial in the school paper protesting the unfairness of the coach's choices.

"Case, don't get so involved," Max warned. "It's all good."

Casey spent the rest of the ride detailing all of Max's football achievements to her friends. Considering that she'd only started going to the games a few weeks ago, her knowledge was quite impressive. But Casey always did her homework. And it was more fun when she was studying her boyfriend. By the time they dropped Emily and Shlepper off, much to Max's embarrassment, she'd convinced Shlepper to feature Max as the cover story in the next edition of the school newspaper.

"That was kinda intense," Max said when they pulled up to her house.

"You think?" Casey was surprised. She thought all good girlfriends gave their boyfriend props. "I'm proud of you. I just want everyone else to know, too."

Max sighed. "I guess it's sweet." He gave her hand a squeeze. "Can I come in?"

As if he needed to ask!

Casey cringed as they entered the living room. Chaos—as usual.

The TV blared. Her stepdad, George, was sitting on

a suitcase, overflowing with clothes. He tried to get the zipper to close.

"George, you're going to call me every night, right?" her mom asked.

"Call you what?" George teased.

Her mom grimaced. She was used to George's wacky sense of humor. "Come on, guys"—she leaned over the sofa and nudged Edwin and Marti—"turn off the TV. Dad's going to Vancouver for three days. Come say good-bye to him."

Edwin hit MUTE, but continued to stare at the screen. "Dad, have a nice time. Bring me back something." He put the volume up again.

Marti ran over to George and wrapped him in a hug.

George had to pry Marti off. His car to the airport honked outside.

"Bye, George," Casey called.

"Good-bye, Casey. Who are *you*?" George asked Max as he lifted his bag.

"Max," Max answered. "Have a good trip."

"Thanks," George said. The driver honked again.

The front door swung open. Derek sauntered in with his arm around Kendra. "That guy in the car's a little hyped, Dad," Derek said. "You better get out there."

George gave Nora a big kiss. "See you," he called and hurried away.

"Rock on," Derek said. "Hey," he gave Max a nod, then led Kendra up the stairs to his room.

"Nice to say hello!" Casey yelled after Derek. Was she suddenly invisible? How rude!

"Hi, Casey," Kendra giggled as Derek pulled her away. Just then, Max's cell phone started buzzing. Casey watched as he quickly read his text message.

"Hey, listen. A bunch of guys are going to Clink's house for an Xbox tournament." Max seemed nervous. "Do you, uh, mind if I go?"

"You want to play a video game? Now? But I thought we were going to hang out." Casey wished her voice didn't sound so shrill.

"He's got the new *Car Wreck* game. It's just out." As if that explained everything.

Casey pouted. She was disappointed.

"I can stay if you want," Max said.

"Oh, go play your video game." Casey pushed him gently toward the door. She had a lab report to write for science anyway. "Promise you'll miss me."

"I promise." He smiled and jogged toward his car. She watched him drive off.

MISS ME YET? she texted a minute later.

MISS ME NOW? she texted five minutes later.

She texted him at least a dozen times that hour. She had a feeling she was getting the hang of this girlfriend thing.

• • • • •

Lizzie dribbled the soccer ball upfield. She scanned the line of defense, searching for a hole. Her feet never stopped moving. The ball was in her control. Out of the corner of her eye, she spotted number 11 pushing toward her. Number 11 was trouble. He was big and fast. She couldn't let him steal the ball. Her team needed one more goal to win.

She sprinted forward, searching, searching . . . until she found Jamie.

Jamie gave her a thumbs-up as he ran along the left side of the field. Lizzie booted the ball to him. Perfect! Jamie dribbled the ball as Lizzie pushed herself through the two remaining defensemen. She set up in front of the goal. Jamie kicked the ball to her. She lined it up and *bam*! She scored!

Jamie raced over to her. *Up, down, slap, slap, snap.* They did their special victory handshake.

Lizzie smiled at her best friend. "We're an awesome team!" she shouted.

Before Jamie could reply, the rest of the guys on their team circled Lizzie. They whooped and cheered for her. They slapped her on the back and punched her arm in celebration.

Lizzie gave all the guys high fives. She loved playing soccer with the Mavericks. She didn't care that she was the only girl on the team. And neither did the boys. Of course, her being the season's highest scorer helped.

"Yay, team!"

"You guys are sooooo good!"

Lizzie glanced toward the sidelines and rolled her eyes. Sophia Wilson and Helen Berger were jumping up and down cheering. *How lame*, Lizzie thought as she wiped the dirt off her knees. She watched as a bunch of guys on the team walked over to them.

The girls giggled and congratulated the guys. They pretended that the guys were too sweaty to talk to and playfully pushed them away. Then they giggled some more. And the guys just stood there, panting like puppies.

She honestly didn't get it. What did they like about them? Sophia and Helen were the ultimate "girly girls." They wore pink spaghetti-strap tank tops and miniskirts with leggings, their hair was always blown out perfectly straight, and they were constantly applying their sparkly lip gloss. Lizzie could never think of anything to say to them—even when they were paired together for school projects. It was as if those girls were from a different planet. A weird, pink, sparkly planet.

"Once again, I come to the rescue!" Jamie boasted as he handed her a bottle of water.

"Oh, please. I was just being nice by passing to you. You looked so bored over there by yourself," Lizzie teased. She and Jamie always teased each other. They had been best friends for years.

"Yeah, right! You were about to be crushed by that big guy going for the ball. If I hadn't been waiting there, you'd be a pancake." Jamie headed to the bench and grabbed his bag.

"Crushed? Never, not me!" Lizzie pulled a sweatshirt over her soccer uniform.

"Hey, Jamie!" called Ethan, a boy on their team. "We're going to get pizza,"—he pointed toward Sophia and Helen—"wanna come?"

"Do you?" Jamie asked Lizzie.

Lizzie wrinkled her nose. "If you want to eat with the girly girls, be my guest. Count me out."

"I'll pass," Jamie told Ethan. Then he pulled one of Lizzie's ponytails. "Race you to your house!" He sprinted away.

Lizzie grabbed her bag and raced after him. She was glad she could count on Jamie to hang with her. At least his brain hadn't been turned to Jell-O by the alien girly girls.

Jamie reached her front door a split second before Lizzie did.

"Winner!" Jamie cried. He pumped his fist in the air.

"You cheat," Lizzie grumbled, wiping the sweat from her forehead.

"Sore loser," Jamie said.

"You're the loser," Lizzie teased. She opened the door. He tossed his bag in the hallway and made himself at home. Jamie was always at her house. They did homework, played games, shot hoops, and took care of all the tropical fish in her aquarium together. Strangers would think she had three new brothers instead of two.

Lizzie flopped down on the living room sofa. Jamie flopped down next to her.

"So you wanna drink?" Lizzie offered.

"I'm good," Jamie said.

"Okay." Lizzie noticed he was twiddling his fingers.

He only did that when he had a test or something made him nervous. "Wanna sneak into Edwin's room and play that cool video game?"

Jamie shrugged. "Maybe later."

"Okay." She watched as his fingers moved around and around. "So what do you want to do?"

"I don't know." He quickly glanced at her and then immediately looked away. "Talk?"

"About what?" Lizzie asked, confused. Jamie wasn't acting like himself. Had something bad happened? Had he failed a test? Come down with a weird tropical disease?

"I don't know," Jamie mumbled. "Stuff."

"What kind of stuff?" Lizzie demanded. "Why are you acting so weird?"

"Uh . . . I think I like you," he blurted out.

Lizzie laughed and relaxed. *That's all?* she thought. "Well, I hope you like me. We hang out every day."

"No. I mean I, like, *like* like you." He stared at her meaningfully.

"Oh . . ." Lizzie was suddenly finding it hard to breathe. "That's a lot of likes."

"Yeah, I know." Jamie started twiddling his fingers again.

Lizzie's brain was spinning. She hopped off the sofa. For some reason it felt weird sitting next to him now. "But it took forever to convince the kids at school that we didn't like each other that way," she said.

"I know," Jamie replied. "I changed my mind."

Lizzie could feel her cheeks turning red. She was angry. Jamie wasn't supposed to do this. Jamie was her *friend*! "Well, you're not allowed to change your mind!" she yelled.

"Oh! I didn't know that!" Jamie yelled back.

"Well, now you do." Lizzie reached over, grabbed his sweatshirt sleeve, and yanked Jamie off the sofa. "So, ah, see you at school tomorrow, okay?" She pushed him toward the front door.

"Ah . . ." Jamie seemed surprised. And very confused.

Lizzie didn't care. He was freaking her out. She had no idea what she was supposed to say to him. She needed him to leave—*now*. "Okay. Bye." She handed him his bag and opened the door.

"Oh." Jamie gazed behind her then blushed.

Lizzie heard footsteps on the stairs and whirled around. *Oh, great!* She cringed as she saw her older sister watching them, her mouth open in surprise. *Casey heard everything!*

"Okay! Bye!" Jamie was suddenly in a hurry to leave. The door clicked shut behind him.

"I swear I wasn't listening," Casey fibbed. Lizzie refused to look at her.

"Okay, well, maybe I kinda heard the good stuff," Casey admitted.

"There was no good stuff," Lizzie grumbled.

"Of course there was," Casey said. "This is so exciting. Jamie wants to be your first boyfriend. He wants to be a couple with you."

"It's not! And he doesn't!" Lizzie cried.

"What do you mean?" Casey asked, obviously not getting the horror of this situation. "It's so romantic! Believe me—and I know—having a boyfriend is so great. I can tell you everything—"

Lizzie couldn't take anymore. She headed up to her room. She was going to hide under her covers until Jamie apologized and everything went back to normal.

"Liz, my door is always open if you want to talk," Casey called after her.

"I'm not talking about this ever again!" Lizzie replied.

• • • • •

"Why's your little sister yelling at Casey?" Kendra asked. Their voices penetrated his closed door, loud and clear.

"Why *wouldn't* you yell at Casey?" Derek retorted. He leaned back in his desk chair and tried to pull Kendra into his lap. She giggled and scooted away.

"Ooh, cute. What's this?" Kendra opened his desk drawer and held up a picture he'd drawn when he was seven.

Derek cringed. He didn't even know why he still owned it. His stick figures were hideous. Their heads were too big for their bodies. "Garbage," Derek said. He snatched the paper, crumpled it into a ball, and made a three-point shot into his trash can.

Woo-hoo! Woo-hoo! Kendra's cell rang with the notes of a Gwen Stefani song.

"Don't answer," Derek said. He tried to pull Kendra in for a kiss.

"As if." Kendra flipped open her hot pink phone. "Hi, Paige. Oh, nothing, I'm just with Derek."

Just with Derek. Great, just great, Derek thought. He had blown off basketball with the guys for the second day in a row, and all she was doing was talking on the phone. He crumpled more paper and practiced his across-the-room shot, while Kendra yapped with her friend.

"Dere, here." Kendra thrust the phone into his hand. He pushed it away.

"Derry, you've got to talk to Paige," Kendra insisted.

"No, I don't," Derek replied.

"Dere-bear, please. Craig is totally ignoring her. She's really sad. You need to cheer her up."

Derek shook his head. He wasn't going to get on the phone and cheer up Paige. "No way," he said again.

She wrapped her arms around him. "Please. She's my best friend. She doesn't have a good boyfriend. You just gotta . . . for me?"

Derek sighed. He found himself sighing a lot lately. "Hand it over." He took the phone. "Hi, Paige," he said in a sickly sweet voice.

Paige spent the next ten minutes listing all the bad things her boyfriend had done, like hanging with his friends, belching, and telling rude jokes. Personally, Derek didn't think Craig had done anything wrong. But judging from the look on Kendra's face, he was wrong, too.

Derek closed his eyes and leaned back. Finally, Paige was off the phone.

"What are you thinking?" Kendra asked.

"That your friend is an idiot?" Derek said.

Kendra gave him a little push. "No, really! What are you really thinking?"

"Nothing," Derek answered honestly. The last hour in his room with Kendra snooping through his desk, gossiping about all the kids at school, and carrying on about Paige's love problems had left his brain dead. Numb.

"You can't be thinking nothing." Kendra was annoyed.

"You don't know me well enough." Derek laughed.

"You never want to share," Kendra argued. "You're not really *in* this relationship."

"Not in this relationship? You've got to be kidding me! All I do is this relationship!" Derek replied.

"What's that supposed to mean?" Kendra countered.

Derek couldn't stop himself. He was on a roll. "It means that we're together all the time. You never give me a break. I never get to spend time with my friends, but you drag me into all your girl stuff, and you know what . . . I'm done. Finished."

"You're breaking up with me?" Kendra asked.

Derek hadn't meant to, but now that it was out there . . .

"Yes," he said.

Kendra burst into tears. Derek gulped. He hated when she cried. She opened his door and swept past Casey, who had obviously been listening in. "You're horrible, Derek Venturi!" Kendra called through her tears.

Derek put his head in his hands. He felt like someone had punched him in the stomach. He wished girls could act like guys. If he had just yelled at a guy like that, the guy would wallop him. Wallop him good. And he'd deserve it. But the punch—no matter how hard—wouldn't hurt as much as making a girl cry.

CHAPTER THREE

Dear Diary,

Everyone in this house is an emotional wreck. Except for me, of course.

My life is great. Max is great. I am great. We are great together.

Derek and Kendra—not so great. In fact, they are OVER. I was walking down the hall when I heard them arguing, so, of course, I listened at the door.

Ever hear of PRIVACY???

Derek was way harsh, but I kind of have to side with him. Kendra had it coming. I mean, a guy like Derek needs his space. Of course, Kendra and Derek do the breakup/makeup thing all the time. I'm sure she'll be back soon.

NO WAY!

But what Derek and Lizzie (who may soon have her

first boyfriend!!!!) don't get is to make a relationship work you gotta be in touch with your own feelings. Of course, the thing about feelings is that they change. That's what makes them so interesting . . . and so painful. But you can't deny your feelings 'cause then you just end up feeling worse.

I've been thinking about how Kendra acted with Derek. Do I act the same with Max? I don't think so.

Reality check—you do! You are the Meddling Queen.

Okay. I'm making a promise—here and now. I will not be a clingy girlfriend. I will be a girlfriend who gives her boyfriend his space. I will be a *perfect* girlfriend.

PERFECT GIRLFRIEND TO DO LIST

1. Let Max hang with his friends. (Maybe I can hang too?) **No, you can't!**

2. Don't call or text too much. (Limit to one time an hour—maybe two?) **Try once or twice a day!**

3. Don't make him spend a lot of time with my family. (Esp. keep away from Derek!)
   Oooh—keep boyfriend away from big, bad wolf Derek!

4. Be interested in football. (Gotta TiVo ESPN!)

5. Try not to talk about tests and grades since I do so much better. **Real nice!**

33

6. Be fun.

How lame! Do you think this is like a test you can study for, Casey?

♡ Love,
Casey

• • • • •

Derek whistled as he walked down the hall. He was in a good mood. A really good mood.

He spotted Ralph at his locker. "Ralphie, my man!" he called. He slam-dunked an imaginary basketball. "We on for hoops later?"

"You know it," Ralph called. "You free to play?"

"Completely free." Derek grinned. It had been several days since he'd broken up with Kendra. And surprisingly, he wasn't sad. All the other times they'd called it quits, he'd been miserable. He'd always missed her. And he guessed she'd missed him, too, because they always got back together *real* fast.

But this time was different. He didn't call Kendra. She didn't call him. They didn't speak in the halls or in the cafeteria. He didn't miss her too much. And, as hard as it was for him to believe, she didn't seem to be missing him at all.

Derek jogged around the kids talking in the hall, weaving his way to his locker. He had so much energy. Without the Kendra drama weighing him down, he felt stronger. Lighter. Happier. He felt like himself again.

There's no way I'm losing this feeling, he vowed.

"Hey, there!" Derek called to his best friend, Sam. They had lockers right near each other.

"Hey!" Sam's blue metal locker was wide open, but he was gazing in the other direction.

"Whassup?" Derek asked, pulling out his binder.

"You think that girl's cute?" Sam pointed down the hall behind Derek.

Derek didn't bother to turn. "No, 'cause I'm not looking."

"She's right over there," Sam said, pointing again.

Derek refused to move. "No, I'm not looking at that girl because I am not looking at girls, period. It's part of my new philosophy."

"You have a philosophy?" Sam asked.

"Mm-hmm." Derek nodded.

Sam rolled his eyes. "Well, give it up, oh, wise Derocrates."

Derek smiled. He liked the new nickname. He *was* kinda like the wise Greek philosopher Socrates—minus the long beard. "Ah, Derocrates decrees that girls are trouble and girlfriends—oooh"—he held up his hands in warning—"are even bigger trouble."

"And you achieved this higher level of understanding how? By dating Kendra for three months?" Sam tapped his fingers on his dark blond hair, as if deep in thought.

"Yes. But the same goes for all girls." Derek was just now coming up with this philosophy. Still, as he explained it to Sam, he realized he was absolutely brilliant. "You see, girls demand to know your thoughts and feelings, and your thoughts about those feelings. But I have absolutely no thoughts . . . about feelings."

Okay, maybe not *totally* brilliant.

"So now that you're done with girls, what are you gonna focus on?" Sam teased. "Your schoolwork?"

Derek laughed. "Ah! Derocrates cares not for books! Derocrates cares only for food and sport." He pounded his chest in a manly way.

Sam didn't respond. He was too busy watching that same red-haired girl down the hall.

"Is girl-watching a sport?" he asked. "Because I could look at Teresa all day."

Derek shook his head. His friend was so weak, so clueless. "Go ahead and waste your time," he said.

"But remember how things worked out with your last girlfriend—what's her name again?"

"Casey?" Sam looked at Derek oddly.

"Yeah." Derek tried to block out that strange time when his best friend had gone over to the dark side and dated his stepsister. "Turned out to be a total time sucker," he reminded Sam.

"Not totally. We're good friends now."

"Great! You can be the cute girl's friend"—Derek nodded toward Teresa—"but don't ask her out. The only way to feel good and live to your full dude potential is to be single."

"Dude!" Sam gave Derek a shove. "Blonde at five o'clock."

Derek didn't move again. "Nice try, Sam, but I will not waste my time turning my head to look at some—"

At that moment, the most beautiful girl Derek had ever seen walked by. She had long, sun-streaked hair, a coppery tan, and amazing blue eyes.

"—good-looking blond girl," he finished meekly. He started to wave to the girl, but quickly stopped himself.

"I'm Derocrates," he said out loud. Now all he had to do was remember the new philosophy that went with his new name: *Girlfriends, feelings, relationships—all trouble!*

• • • • •

Lizzie visited the nurse right before lunch. She didn't feel sick—at least not the kind of sick Mrs. McGee could cure. But she pretended to have a headache.

She knew the drill. The gray-haired school nurse popped a thermometer under her tongue, then asked when was the last time she ate. Kids never got sent home for a headache. Lizzie told Mrs. McGee she forgot to eat breakfast. The nurse diagnosed her as hungry and hurried her off to the cafeteria. Ten minutes late. Perfect.

Lizzie had been working hard the past couple of days to avoid Jamie. It wasn't easy to hide from your best friend. But Lizzie just couldn't think of a better plan.

"Lizzie! Over here!"

She knew Jamie had spotted her, but she pretended she didn't hear him.

She scanned the blue-tiled cafeteria. She had to make a choice. Fast. She couldn't let herself be forced to her usual table with Jamie and all the soccer guys. It would be way too weird.

Sophia Wilson pushed past her, carrying two big bottles of diet peach iced tea.

"Sophia!" Lizzie quickly called out.

Sophia turned, her green eyes wide with confusion. Lizzie hadn't actually talked to Sophia since an after-school art class they both took in the third grade.

"Hey, Sophia," Lizzie pushed on. "Can I ask you a question about the English homework?"

"Uh, sure." Sophia gave her a strange look, then continued to her table.

Lizzie followed, as if she'd been invited. She could feel Jamie watching her from across the room. Without asking, she squeezed onto the bench, next to Sophia and across from Helen.

"What's your question?" Sophia asked. She tucked a piece of her blond hair behind her ear.

"Question?" Lizzie was startled. "Oh, yeah, about English." Lizzie unwrapped her sandwich and tried to come up with one. "Uh, were there nine or ten vocab words to define?"

"Ten." Sophia giggled. They'd been having ten words a week since the beginning of school.

Lizzie nodded and focused on her sandwich. Sophia and Helen didn't seem to mind that she was there. In fact, they completely ignored her. She listened to them talk about their new mulberry lip gloss. She learned that fuchsia slim cut jeans were arriving today at the mall. She watched them flirt with the nearby table of boys. They both thought Rod Morrow was supercute. They giggled about the way his black hair fell over his eyes. Lizzie snuck a quick glance at Rod. The boy was in sore need of a haircut.

Lizzie cringed. She didn't belong here. She belonged at her usual table with Jamie. Telling bad knock-knock jokes. Coming up with strategies for that week's soccer match. Bragging about her new video game high score.

I can't go back, Lizzie realized. Jamie had ruined it. Ruined it with three horrible words.

She crumpled the foil from her sandwich. Sophia and Helen would probably be so excited if a boy said he liked them. They'd probably run out and buy a new dress. Or a new lip gloss. But the thought of Jamie liking her—well, it made her feel kinda sick. Almost like everything was spinning way too fast.

Why can't I be like other girls? Lizzie wondered. *What's wrong with me?*

"Why aren't you sitting with the boys?" Helen finally asked.

"Dunno," Lizzie replied. "Not in the boy mood."

"I'm always in the boy mood!" Sophia exclaimed with a giggle.

"Why aren't you in a boy mood?" Helen asked. She seemed genuinely interested. "You act like a boy."

"What's that supposed to mean?" Lizzie shot back.

"You always wear pants and those sports jerseys. You play soccer on a boys' team. All your friends are boys," Helen recited matter-of-factly.

Lizzie was about to say something nasty but stopped herself. Helen hadn't said anything that wasn't true. Lizzie never really thought about it like that before. *Maybe I'm the problem,* Lizzie realized. *Maybe I should try to act more like Helen and Sophia and the other giggly girls at this table.*

"Not anymore," Lizzie announced. She ran her fingers through her low ponytails. "I was thinking of getting my hair cut. Any suggestions?"

She'd said the magic words. Within seconds, Helen and Sophia had whisked Lizzie to the girls' room for a makeover.

The bell for class rang a short while later.

"Oh, you look so cute!" Sophia giggled. She gave Lizzie kisses on both cheeks. She thought this was very chic.

"Now you're totally one of us," Helen gushed. "See you at the mall later, okay?" She waved as she hurried with Sophia to class.

41

Lizzie stared at herself in the mirror. Her brown hair—out of its usual ponytails—was poufed and held back with a rhinestone headband. Her skin shimmered with glittery body lotion and her mouth glistened with lip gloss. Long sparkly earrings dangled from her ears, and she smelled like Sophia's flowery perfume.

I look like the girly girls, she realized in horror. *I look like the kind of girl that boys like.*

She felt like a fool.

Grabbing a handful of paper towels, she rubbed her skin raw, removing all traces of the makeup.

She wasn't going shopping with the giggly twins for pink jeans at the mall this afternoon—that was for sure. But she wasn't going to play soccer with Jamie either. She was going back to her original plan. She would ignore Jamie. A freeze-out. Then Jamie would either leave her alone for good, or his feelings for her would change back to normal.

Either way—problem solved.

CHAPTER FOUR

Casey sat at the dining room table, her history book and notebook spread out before her. But her eyes kept drifting over to the living room, where Marti lay on the sofa, surrounded by ten stuffed animals, watching cartoons.

Oh, I love that one! Casey thought. She twisted her body so she had a better view of the superhero cat, but she kept her pen in writing position on the paper. It made her feel like she was doing homework.

"Hey, Marti!" Lizzie called as she bounded down the stairs. "Got room for one more?" She flopped onto the sofa.

Six-year-old Marti looked at her stepsister in surprise. "You want to watch cartoons with us? Cool!" She grinned widely. "Who do you want to sit next to?"

Lizzie surveyed all of Marti's furry friends. "How about . . . Gomer the Gecko?"

Marti handed Lizzie the huge blue gecko with red spots. "Good choice!"

Lizzie laid the stuffed lizard over her lap as the phone rang.

Casey jumped up to answer it, but Edwin appeared out of nowhere, snatching the receiver off the living room side table before she was anywhere near it.

"Hello?" Edwin's face fell. It obviously wasn't for him. "Sure. Hold on."

He walked over to the sofa. "Hey, Lizzie. It's Jamie." He thrust the receiver toward her.

"Tell him I'll call back," she said, never taking her eyes off the TV screen. "I'm watching TV with a gecko."

Edwin gave Lizzie a quizzical look. Lizzie used to spend half the afternoon talking to Jamie on the phone. Sisters were hard to figure out! He sat in the overstuffed armchair. "Hey, Jamie," he said into the phone. "Here's an excuse you don't get too often. She can't talk now 'cause she's watching cartoons with a gecko."

Lizzie gasped. She hurled the lizard at Edwin.

Edwin ducked and laughed. "That's what I said. Later, Jamie."

As Casey watched Lizzie stare at the TV, she tried to figure out what her sister was thinking. Was she playing hard to get? Was she angry with Jamie? Maybe she was just really into the superhero cat.

Twenty minutes later the phone rang again. It was Jamie.

"He's baaaack!" Edwin laughed then covered the receiver. "He wants to talk to you, Lizzie," he whispered.

"I can't. I'm busy." Lizzie stood and hurried toward the stairs.

"She's still busy," Edwin told Jamie. Then he followed Lizzie to the stairs. "Hey, look. If you're gonna break Jamie's heart you should get it over with. Don't leave him hanging."

Lizzie whirled around. "Did Casey tell you?"

"I would never," Casey called.

"No, I eavesdropped," Edwin admitted.

"Ugh! Can't anyone have a private conversation in this house?" Lizzie cried.

"Well, maybe Marti," joked Edwin. "She's kind of off in her own world."

"Lucky her!" Lizzie hurried to her room and slammed the door.

"Whoa! What's with her?" Edwin raised his arms in surrender.

Casey stood and jogged up the stairs. "Girl stuff," she explained. "Time for big sis to the rescue."

Casey knocked cautiously. Lizzie wasn't usually a door-slammer. Something big was going on.

"Enter," Lizzie grumbled.

Casey pushed open the door. Lizzie sat on her bright orange comforter cleaning her shoes. She twisted a popsicle stick back and forth to loosen the dirt from the bottom of her soccer cleat. Casey watched a hunk of dirt fall into the small wastebasket below the bed.

"Shouldn't you do that in the mudroom?" Casey asked.

"Probably." Lizzie didn't look up. She pushed her braids out of her eyes and dug out more mud.

"Okay, then!" Casey said brightly. "I just came to say good night."

Lizzie turned. "No, you came to talk about Jamie."

"Jamie? Jamie?" Casey pretended to be searching her memory. "Now why does that name sound so familiar?"

"Because he's my friend. Who told me he liked me."

"Oh, that Jamie!" Casey sat at the end of the bed and tucked her legs under her. "I like that Jamie."

"Yeah, so did I. But now I can't stand that Jamie." Lizzie pounded out her confusion on the cleat. Bits of mud sprayed on the carpet.

"Why?" Casey asked.

"Because all those times we played soccer, ate pizza, hung out as friends—it was all a lie!" Lizzie cried.

Casey rested her hand on her sister's arm to stop the angry hacking at the cleat. "Liz, you can't be mad at Jamie for liking you."

Lizzie yanked her arm away. "Yes, I can."

"But why can't someone be your friend and like you, too?" Casey reasoned.

"Because I don't know how to talk to him anymore!" Lizzie exploded. "I don't even want to see him."

"Okay." Casey decided to try another approach. "Well, maybe you're just not ready for a boyfriend."

"Maybe I am ready!" Tears collected in the corner of Lizzie's eyes. She gulped them back.

"Okay, maybe you are," Casey agreed hesitantly. *What am I supposed to say?* Casey wondered, eyeing the door for a quick escape. *Should I get Mom?* Her mom definitely had more experience with this confusing heart-to-heart stuff than she did. "Maybe Jamie's not the right guy for you," Casey tried. "Maybe you like someone else."

Lizzie smiled. "You're right! That's it! I like someone else."

"You do?" Casey squealed. She couldn't help herself. This was definitely a conversation she could get into now.

"Who?"

"Who?" Lizzie repeated.

"Come on, you can tell your sister. Who is he?" Casey couldn't control her excitement.

"Uh . . . Rod." Lizzie nodded. "He's in my class, he's on the swim team, and all the girls think he's really cute."

Casey hugged her sister. "That's great! Poor Jamie."

Lizzie frowned. "Poor me! I just lost my best friend."

"C'mon, Liz, you don't have to lose him. If you tell him you like another guy, then you two will go back to being friends," Casey said. "But you do have to talk to him."

"But how can I talk to him if I can't even look at him?" Lizzie sighed and flopped back onto her bed.

"Don't worry." Casey leaned over and tickled Lizzie to make her laugh. "It'll work out."

• • • • •

Derek glanced at the clock on the dashboard. *I'm late . . . again,* he realized.

He parked his car behind Smelly Nelly's and hurried through the back door and into the kitchen of the café. He was immediately greeted by the aroma of cinnamon from the fresh baked goods and the faint smell of garlic and sesame seeds from Nelly's famous hummus. Smelly

Nelly's was a hip, vegetarian café. No meat and few animal by-products were served. But the cool thing was that if the customer wasn't up for tofu and carrot juice, he could also order milkshakes and cake.

"Hey, Carlos!" Derek greeted one of the cooks.

"Nice of you to come to work," Carlos said. He stir-fried soba noodles over the grill.

Derek pinned his gold name tag on his black Smelly Nelly's shirt. The T-shirt featured a cartoon of a silly cat. He'd been working here for several months. Working definitely wasn't his favorite thing. But his dad wouldn't spring for gas money for his car, so it didn't leave him a choice. He grabbed an order pad and pushed open the swinging door to the restaurant.

"Ow!" A blond-haired girl, who'd been going the other way, held her elbow where the door had banged it.

Derek stared at her, stunned. She was gorgeous. She looked as if she should be holding a surfboard on a beach somewhere. Then he recognized her. She was the new girl he'd spotted in the hall with Sam.

"Hey"—he looked at her name tag—"Sally. Guess you're the new girl." Derek smiled.

"And you're the late guy," Sally said, ignoring his knock-a-girl-over smile. She ripped off an order from her pad. "Here," she said, handing him the paper. "I kindly picked up table ten's order for you."

"Oh, thanks."

Stop. Stop right now. Derek was dimly aware of his brain trying to communicate with him. Reminding him that girls were trouble.

"No, don't thank me. Just don't expect me to pick up any of your slack," Sally said. She still hadn't smiled back at him.

"Oh, don't worry, you won't have to," Derek assured her. He couldn't believe what an attitude this girl had. She sounded just like Casey!

Sally shook her head. "Yeah? That's not what I hear."

"Heard what from whom?" Derek asked.

"From Beth." She gave him a look that said I-know-all-the-dirt-and-it-ain't-pretty.

"A-ha! You know Beth?" Derek tried to sound surprised. Innocent.

"I know Beth. She's my best friend."

Not good, Derek realized. Beth was one of Smelly Nelly's former waitresses. He and Beth had dated briefly before he was with Kendra, and it had ended badly.

"So don't think your cute smile and fake messy hair is gonna work with me, because I'm not here to flirt like she was," Sally warned. "I'm here to work."

"Yeah?" Derek said, rising to the challenge. "Well, so am I!" He pulled a pen out of his pocket to show he meant business.

Sally shrugged and headed into the kitchen. Totally blowing him off.

"And, for your information, my hair is naturally messy!" Derek called after her. He ran his fingers through his hair.

Girls are trouble. Girls are trouble, he repeated to himself.

He managed to avoid her for a full half hour, even though the café was small. Dinnertime was busy. He was juggling four tables at once—getting their food, refilling their drinks, and answering questions about the menu.

He grabbed one of his orders from Carlos and hurried out of the kitchen.

"What's that?" Sally demanded, suddenly standing in front of him.

Derek couldn't get over how incredible-looking she was. Even the Smelly Nelly's T-shirt looked hot on her. "It's a bulgur burger, and yes, it tastes as bad as it sounds."

Sally didn't laugh. She didn't even crack a smile. "Have you seen my large hummus?"

"Excuse me?"

"My large hummus," Sally repeated. "You know, that chickpea and sesame dip. I ordered it, like, twenty minutes ago."

Derek gave a little shrug and a pout that he knew all the girls loved. "Oh, sorry. I thought it was my large hummus. I gave it to table ten."

Sally didn't react to his shrug and pout. *What's with her?* Derek wondered. He was intrigued. Usually girls were totally into him by now. It was part of his charm.

She reached out and grabbed the plate he was holding. "I'll just take this instead."

Derek held the plate tightly. "No, you won't! I ordered that a half hour ago."

"You should have thought of that before you grabbed the hummus," Sally shot back.

"That's my burger!" Cute or not, Sally was not gonna mess up his tips tonight. He needed that money. Gas was crazy expensive.

A bell rang. "One large hummus is up!" Carlos called from the kitchen.

Sally released the burger. "There you go. I think that's yours." She walked into the kitchen to claim her food.

Derek watched her go . . . until the guy at table six waved frantically for his burger.

Two hours later, they were done for the night. All the customers were gone. Sally wiped down the tables. Derek swept the crumbs from the floor. He glanced at her as he worked. She was amazing. Earlier, she'd dropped a pitcher of iced tea. The pitcher shattered, ice cubes spilled on the customer, and their boss had let her have it. But she didn't cry. She didn't come whining to him. She didn't even get upset. She just cleaned up the mess and continued on.

Amazing.

"So do you guys pool tips here?" Sally suddenly asked. "I did pretty well tonight."

"No. But I did pretty well, too." Derek wanted to make sure that she knew that he was actually good at his job, even if he wasn't always on time to work.

"I'm sure you did." Sally laughed.

"What's that supposed to mean?" Derek asked.

"How many girls did you hit on?" she asked.

"None! I don't do that anymore," Derek said. "It's part of my new 'date-free/feeling good' philosophy."

"Oh, really?" Sally raised her eyebrows. "Beth didn't tell me you're the philosophical type. But now I know why you didn't ask me out. I was starting to get a little insulted."

Derek stopped sweeping. "Did you want me to ask you out?"

"No, I don't think my boyfriend would be that into it," she said.

Boyfriend? Derek was startled. *It's better,* he realized. *She's taken and I'm not dating anymore.*

"Works for me. I'm a changed man," he declared.

"Why?" Sally asked. "Did you get your heart broken?"

"No," Derek said. He shut the lights and they headed for the door. "I just don't have one."

• • • • •

This is bad, Derek realized. He gazed at the green numbers on his digital clock. 3:12 A.M.

He closed his eyes. Tried to sleep.

Sally. All he saw was Sally.

Her hair. Her eyes. Her tan. The woven bracelet on her wrist. Her confidence. Well, he couldn't actually *see* her confidence, but he knew it was there.

Derek couldn't stop thinking about Sally. All night.

He hardly knew her. Did she like hip-hop or rock? Did she like mint chocolate chip ice cream? Suddenly these things seemed *really* important.

Derek threw off the comforter and scrambled out of bed. He needed a distraction. Needed to get his head back to his 'no girls' philosophy.

In fifteen minutes, he was settled on the sofa in the dark living room. A soccer match from some South American country on the TV. A bowl of potato chips in his lap. Edwin by his side.

Edwin yawned again. "Derek? I still don't get it. What am I doing here? Why'd you drag me out of bed at three in the morning?"

"It's never too late for some brotherly bonding," Derek said. He passed the chips to Edwin.

Edwin pushed them away. "Are you having girl troubles and you need some company to distract you?"

Is it that obvious? Derek wondered. He shoved a handful of chips in his mouth. He wondered what Sally was thinking about. Probably nothing. She was probably sleeping.

Edwin pushed Derek with his foot. "What's her name?"

Derek stared bleary-eyed at the screen. "Just eat and watch sports, okay, Sally?"

"Did you just call me *Sally*?" Edwin laughed.

"No!" Derek groaned. He turned up the volume of the Spanish-speaking sportscaster. It was gonna be a long night.

CHAPTER FIVE

Dear Diary,

Lizzie likes a boy! This is so exciting. It's a whole new adventure for her—and she's shared it with ME. I need to help her. But what can I do? **Butt out!**

I know! Lizzie is way too shy to flirt with Rod. I mean, she can't even talk to her best friend and she doesn't even have feelings for him. I need to seek out Rod for her. Drop some hints. Make him realize that Lizzie is the girl for him. If I get Rod to ask Lizzie out, she'll be so happy. And she'll never have to know it was me. I'll be so sneaky . . .

Yeah, good plan. You can barely flirt yourself and now you want to flirt for other people? Unreal . . .

♡ Love,
Casey

• • • • •

"Guess who."

Casey smiled as the warm hands covered her eyes. She immediately knew it was Max. She'd been missing him since lunch. They didn't have any classes together in the afternoon.

"Is it Principal Henderson?" Casey played along.

"Nope. He's not nearly as good-looking as I am!"

Casey giggled. "Oh, then it must be Emily!"

"Do these hands feel like girl hands?" Max exclaimed, outraged.

Casey spun around. "Of course not!" She gave him a hug, but pulled back when she spotted Derek coming down the hall making a gagging sign.

"Wanna go get some ice cream? I have enough cash for a hot fudge sundae," Max offered.

Casey loved ice cream, and, well, anything with hot fudge had her name written all over it. "Yeah . . . actually, no." At that moment, she noticed Max's football buddies passing a foam football across the hall. "I mean, don't you have practice?"

Max shut her locker for her. "Late practice tonight. We've got time for a quick scoop."

Casey eyed Derek hanging with Sam and Ralph. Then she overheard Max's football buddies planning to grab a slice of pizza. She remembered her vow not to be a clingy girlfriend. *Might as well start now,* she realized.

"You go hang with your friends," she said.

"Really?" Max seemed surprised.

"Really. Besides, I have something I need to do." Casey headed for the front door.

"What?" Max asked, walking alongside her.

"Well, you see, Lizzie and Jamie—" Casey quickly stopped herself. She could hear Derek's voice echoing in her head: *Too much info. Don't drag him into your dramas.* "It's nothing. Just crazy family stuff." Casey waved it off.

Max shrugged. "Okay. Actually, my mom was really crazy this morning."

"What happened?" Casey asked.

"The garbage truck was turning around on our dead-end street. The guy kinda missed and ran over part of our lawn with his huge tires. My mom went ballistic, tearing out into the road in her pajamas and slippers," Max reported.

"Oh, no! She didn't! Then what happened?" Casey asked.

"She got into this big fight with the garbage guy. Screaming on our front lawn."

"Were you totally embarrassed?"

"Not until the garbage guy's mutt hopped out of the

truck and began peeing on our lawn. My mom screeched so loudly that the neighbors ran out of their houses," Max said, laughing.

"How horrible. What did the neighbors say? What did you—?" Casey stopped mid-question. Max's friends were waiting impatiently by the door. She realized that she was asking too many questions. She should let him go. Give him space. She remembered what had happened between Derek and Kendra. "You know, I need to leave," she fibbed.

"B-but—" Max sputtered.

"Tell me the rest later." Casey gave Max a quick peck on his cheek and pushed him toward his buddies.

I am an amazing girlfriend, Casey congratulated herself as she walked down the block. She stopped in front of the community center. She had a great idea.

She pushed open the double glass doors and hurried down the tiled hall, the heavy smell of chlorine following her. She knew that the school swim teams practiced at the community center pool. And Lizzie had said Rod was a swimmer. *Am I good or am I good?* Casey thought.

Warm, sticky air surrounded her as she stepped through the doors to the pool. Rows and rows of swimmers cut through the blue water, doing laps. She felt ridiculously overdressed in her cords and sweater. A trickle of sweat worked its way down her neck.

Casey made her way over to the metal bleachers by the side of the Olympic-sized pool. And realized she had two problems.

Even if Rod was there, she had no idea what he looked like.

And she had no clue what to say to make an eleven-year-old boy ask out her sister.

First things first. She scanned the pool. How to find Rod? All the boys underwater in their navy trunks and wet hair looked the same. Then she heard a giggle and knew she had her answer.

She slid to the end of the bleachers, right next to two giggling girls who looked to be about Lizzie's age. With their glossy lips and overly styled hair, these girls were watching the boys swim with such intensity that Casey knew she'd found her informants.

"Rod's a good swimmer, isn't he?" Casey said casually.

"Ohh, he's the best!" the dark-haired groupie gushed.

"Which one is he again?" Casey squinted, pretending she had trouble seeing.

"Duh! He's, like, the guy way ahead of all the others," her blond friend giggled. She pointed to the far lane.

"Thanks." Casey hurried across the pool. She squatted down at the end of Rod's lane.

Rod glided through the water, pulling forward with an effortless freestyle. Just as his fingers grazed the wall and he was about to flip-turn, Casey leaned over to tap him. Too hard! Her tap was more like a smack, and the force plunged Rod under the water.

"Oh!" Casey leaped up.

"What the—?" Rod sputtered as he surfaced.

"Sorry," Casey apologized. "Just wanted to talk."

"Now?" He gazed at his teammates finishing their laps. "Who are you?"

Casey thought about telling the truth, but that sounded too lame. A tall guy with large biceps and a whistle around his neck eyed her suspiciously from across the pool. The coach. "I'm, uh, a reporter for the high school paper. We want to do a story about you."

Rod smiled and slicked his black hair away from his piercing blue eyes. "Just about me, huh?" He puffed out his chest.

Casey relaxed. This was going to be easy. "All about you. Can I ask you some questions?"

"Right now?" Rod glanced at his coach. "How about after practice?"

Casey checked out the coach. A kid with a leg cramp hobbled over to him, distracting him. She knew she had to work fast before the coach was onto her. "No, I gotta do it now. Deadline, you know. So, uh, how long have you been swimming?"

"Since I was seven. I've always been really fast in the water." Rod rested his forearms on the side of the pool. "Where's your notepad?"

"Notepad?" Casey watched the coach massage the kid's cramped calf.

"Aren't you writing this down? For the article?"

"Oh, right." Casey opened her school bag and rummaged around. No blank paper. She pulled out her MP3 player. "This is also a tape recorder," she fibbed. She pressed a button.

"Cool. Gotta get me one of those," Rod said.

"So, do you have a girlfriend?" Casey asked.

"Girlfriend? That's in the article?"

"Sure!" Casey nodded enthusiastically. "Your fans want to know *everything* about you."

Rod smiled and puffed his chest some more. "I'm single . . . and lookin' for love."

Casey couldn't believe Lizzie was crushing on this conceited airhead. "What kind of girls do you like?"

"You know, pretty, fun, cute—that kinda stuff." Rod ran his fingers through his hair again. "Is there a photographer coming to take my picture?"

"Photographer?" Casey could feel the water from the tiles seeping through the knees of her pants. "Oh . . . he's coming later." The coach was eyeing her again. "What do you think of Lizzie McDonald?"

"Lizzie?" Rod was completely confused.

"Morrow!" the coach bellowed across the pool. "Time for sprints. Move it!"

"Meet you at the other end," Rod said to Casey. He sped through the water.

Casey tossed the MP3 player into her bag, then ran alongside his lane to the other end of the pool. Her heavy book bag thudded against her damp wool sweater.

Rod popped his head up from the water. "Why Lizzie?" he asked.

"I'm doing an article on her, too," Casey panted.

"Yeah, she plays soccer," Rod said. "She's cool."

"Morrow!" the coach barked. "Swim!"

Rod dove under the water. Like a bullet out of a gun, he was halfway across the pool in seconds. Casey raced to keep up with him. Sweat plastered her long hair to her cheeks. *If Lizzie only knew what I was doing for her,* Casey thought.

At the end of the lane, Casey asked Rod, "Do you like her?"

"You mean *like* like her?"

"Yeah," Casey said eagerly.

"Hey, you!" The coach pointed at Casey.

Rod pushed off the wall, pumping his arms through the water. Casey heaved as she sprinted back to the other end. Her heart pounded. The coach was making his way toward her.

Rod surfaced.

"Well?" Casey wheezed.

"Lizzie's cute," he said.

Score! She was on her way to getting Lizzie and Rod together.

"Lizzie likes you, too," she blurted.

"Miss, you need to leave. You're disrupting practice." The coach towered above Casey.

"No problem." Casey stood to go.

"Hey! What about the photographer?" Rod called after her.

"I'll get back to you," Casey promised.

• • • • •

Derek secretly sniffed his armpits.

Casey and Derek

Max—Casey's boyfriend

Casey tries so hard to be the perfect girlfriend.

Derek and Kendra—
breaking up is hard to do!

Casey gives Lizzie advice
at Smelly Nelly's.

Sally has to choose. Will she pick Patrick or Derek?

Sally—Derek's dream girl

Nope. Nothing—just the faint aroma of that citrus soap Nora had put in the shower. Not that he really thought he smelled, but it never hurt to check once in a while.

Then what's wrong? he wondered.

He'd been working all night with Sally. He'd used his best lines, his best smiles, and even cracked a few of his best jokes. But nothing. She seemed to like him okay, but she just wasn't into him. He knew he shouldn't care. He'd sworn off girls. But he never met a girl that he couldn't charm—and Casey didn't count because she was like a weird breed of girl.

It bothered him that cute Sally didn't like him.

And it bothered him that it bothered him.

It's the boyfriend, he reasoned. *The boyfriend is messing her up.*

At least that made some kind of sense.

Derek sighed. He'd been right from the beginning. Girls were trouble.

"See ya," Derek called to the last customers of the night. He practically had to pick the couple up and carry them to the door. Didn't they realize that he wanted to go home and chill on the sofa?

He locked the door. He flipped over the CLOSED sign

in the window of Smelly Nelly's so the cartoon cat was now waving good-bye.

"Finally!" Derek said to Sally. "Crazy busy tonight, huh?"

He glanced across the café. Sally sat at an empty table, talking on her cell. She seemed really into her conversation.

"Whatever," Derek grumbled. He found the broom and began the nightly sweep up. He could hear Carlos scrubbing down the kitchen.

"How many times should I say it?" Sally raised her voice.

Derek wondered who was on the phone.

"It's not going to work out." Sally sounded angry. "Look, it's over. Just forget it. Yeah, fine. Bye."

Sally flicked her cell closed and shoved it in the back pocket of her jeans. She grabbed one of the wooden chairs and heaved it onto the table with a slam.

Whoa, she's angry! "I know you're new, but we try not to break chairs here," Derek joked.

"My boyfriend and I just had a fight." Sally stacked another chair on the table. Every night all the chairs were put up so the floor could be cleaned.

Derek held up his hands. "Sorry! Not my field of expertise."

Oh, no! Here it comes. The big sob story, Derek thought.

"Patrick doesn't call me for a week and he's all, like, 'How come you're not free?'" Sally continued to lift the chairs onto the small round tables. "How does he think that makes me feel?"

Derek stopped sweeping. "Are you asking me? 'Cause I don't do relationships and I don't talk relationships."

"You know, I should have dumped that guy weeks ago!" Sally shook her head, as if to clear it from the bad vibe of the boyfriend. Then she turned to him and asked cheerfully, "Hey, can I have a ride home?"

"Wait, uh, that's it?" Derek asked. "You're over it? Just like that?"

Sally shrugged. "Yeah."

He had never seen a girl break up with her boyfriend so calmly. *Where was the crying? The drama?* "Wow. I can't say I've ever met a girl like you."

Sally finally smiled at him and shrugged. "Yeah. Well, I'm gonna get changed. I'll see you out front."

Amazing, Derek thought, his mood brightening. *This girl is amazing.*

The next morning, Derek hurried to his locker. He was late. As usual.

Sam was standing by his own locker with the cute red-haired girl from the other day. She handed him a notebook. "Thanks," Sam said, his eyes never straying from Teresa's face. "So I'll see you Saturday?"

"Yeah. I'll see you!" Teresa gave a flirty little wave and ran off to meet her girlfriends down the hall.

"Saturday?" Derek asked, twirling his combination lock.

"It's not what you think," Sam said defensively.

"I think you asked her out."

Sam nodded. "Okay, it's exactly what you think. I'm guilty. Give me the I-told-you-so speech. Tell me how I ignored your philosophy, Derocrates."

Derek pulled some books out of his messy locker. He waved Sam off. "C'mon, you know I was just kidding about the whole 'no girls, no girlfriend' philosophy. We're dudes! Dudes need girls."

Sam smirked. They'd been friends for too long. He knew what Derek's change of philosophy meant. "What's her name?" he asked.

"Sally. She's a new waitress at the restaurant."

"She cute?" Sam asked, leaning in for the details.

"Very! And get this—when she has a problem, she just fixes it—herself! She doesn't go on and on about her problems." Derek thought about how different Sally was from Kendra. "She's kinda like a guy!"

Sam took a step back. "Huh?"

"But she's all woman!" Derek quickly added.

"That's cool," Sam agreed. "So she sounds great. When are you asking her out?"

"Well, she just dumped her boyfriend, so . . . minus one . . ."—Derek pretended to do a complicated math problem on an imaginary blackboard—"I'll give her a couple of days and then turn on the charm."

"Nice." Sam raised his palm and they did their dude handshake.

Relationships aren't bad, Derek decided. *Relationships with the wrong kind of girl are what's bad. And I've been dating the wrong girls.*

Sally was going to be different.

CHAPTER SIX

Casey traced the A at the top of the paper with her finger. No matter how many times she got them, it always felt good. Kind of magical. She carefully tucked the math test into her binder as she made her way to her next class.

She heard Max's voice long before she saw him. "I can't believe Mrs. Ashton took five points off for that. She messed up my grade," he complained loudly to Clink.

Casey winced. Max had Mrs. Ashton for math the period before she did. He must be talking about the test. She wondered if she should go over and ask how he did. But then he'd want to know how she did. And he might think she was bragging. Perfect girlfriends didn't do that.

She froze, frantically searching the hallway for Emily or someone. Anyone. She needed to change her course.

If she met Max at their usual spot before fourth period, she'd have to talk about the test. Right in front of his super-popular friend Clink, too. She knew it was a recipe for relationship disaster.

A-ha! Paul would hide her. Casey hurried across the hall and flung herself into the guidance office. Paul, the guidance counselor, always came to her rescue. His office was like a second home.

"Casey!" Paul looked up from his computer, startled as she barreled into his office. She slammed the door shut and flopped into one of the gray armchairs in front of his desk.

"Nice to knock." Paul shook his head in amazement. "I could have had a student in here, talking to me about his problems."

"But you don't," Casey countered. She gazed at the door, calculating her plan. The bell would ring in a few minutes. Max would figure she got hung up somewhere and go to class. Then she could wheedle a pass out of Paul and go to history class late.

Paul leaned back, stretching his long, lanky legs under his desk. He was in his early thirties and pretty cool for someone who worked in a high school. "Who are you hiding from?"

"Me? Hiding?" Casey gave a laugh that sounded fake, even to her.

"Yeah, you." Paul reached into his desk drawer and pulled out a bag of corn chips. He popped one in his mouth and handed the open bag to Casey. He knew Casey liked corn chips. She visited him a lot.

"I'm not hiding. Just avoiding my boyfriend." Casey nibbled on a chip.

"Oh, so you two are having a fight. That's rough."

"No! Max and I are so happy together. Everything's great!" Casey said.

"If things are great between a girl and her boyfriend, then why would she hide from him?" Paul asked.

"I told you I'm *not* hiding. I'm giving him space," Casey explained.

"He wants space from you?"

"No!" Sometimes Casey wondered how Paul got his guidance counselor degree or whatever it was called. He always seemed two steps behind her. "He doesn't know he wants space. He'll never want space, because I'm already giving him space."

"And you're doing this because why?" Paul wrinkled his forehead in confusion and scratched his curly black hair.

"Because I'm the perfect girlfriend."

"Of course." Paul smiled as if he'd just heard a joke.

"Really. You see, any girl can like a guy," Casey explained. "But the trick is to show the guy you like that you really like him by not showing him all the time that you do like him."

"I'm not following," Paul admitted as the bell for class rang.

"Relationships are tricky, Paul," Casey warned as she stood to go. "May I have a pass? I don't want to be too late."

Paul handed her a pink pass. "Barge in any time, Casey. You brighten my day."

• • • • •

Lizzie scooted closer to the TV. Things were heating up between Sarah and Olivier in *Dark River Falls*. She loved this soap opera. The characters were so good-looking, and their lives were so wild. Nothing like her life.

Until recently.

Until Olivier told Sarah he had deep feelings for her.

Sarah: Olivier, I care about you. Just not that way.

Olivier: Sarah, you know you are in love with me!

"Gross," Marti moaned, next to her. "Can we watch cartoons? This is boring."

"Shhh!" Lizzie turned up the volume.

Sarah: But, Olivier, that's not true!

Olivier: Then kiss me and find out.

Lizzie sat open-mouthed as brooding Olivier gathered frail Sarah in his arms. He leaned her back for a dramatic kiss.

"Ewww! I don't want to find out!" Marti covered her face with the sofa cushion.

Visions of Jamie popped into her mind. Lizzie felt sick. "Me, neither!" she agreed.

Sarah sighed on-screen, as Olivier brought his lips closer and closer.

Sarah: Oh! I must tell—

"Hey, chickpeas. Anything good on?" Lizzie's mom perched on the arm of the sofa.

"No," Marti said. She pressed the clicker and the screen instantly turned black.

"Marti!" Lizzie cried. "Sarah was just about to tell Olivier he was married to her sister before she married his doctor!"

"I didn't know you watched soap operas." Her mom sounded surprised.

Lizzie felt her cheeks turn red. "Oh yeah, they're really funny. All that love stuff is so *funny*." She didn't want her mom to know she was kind of watching them to figure out how all that love stuff worked. If she said that, she was sure her mom would pull out some embarrassing book and want to have a long talk. No thanks.

"I don't think it's funny, because I have a crush on Zach in my class," Marti piped up.

"You do?" Lizzie and her mom said together.

"Yeah. Naomi likes him, too, and she's my best friend, but we talked and it's okay," Marti reported matter-of-factly.

Lizzie's mom gave Marti a hug. "I didn't know you liked boys."

"Just the cute ones," Marti replied.

"You know, I thought your dad was so cute when I first met him," she said. "Of course, I didn't know until later that I liked him."

"So, ummm . . . when did you figure that out?" Lizzie hoped her question sounded like she didn't really care. But maybe her mom did have some wisdom to share . . .

"Actually, it was right there," Nora said, gesturing toward the dining room. "We'd been dating for a few weeks, and he decided to make me a special dinner."

Lizzie nodded. She remembered when her mom started dating George. She was so happy. Lizzie and Casey hadn't seen her in a really good mood since she'd divorced their dad.

"George cooked salmon. He was really nervous. He kept making these bad fish jokes. It was cute." She had a far-away look in her eyes as she recalled the fateful date.

"And then what happened?" Lizzie asked.

"Well, it was the first time we talked about our families meeting each other. So I knew he was serious about me," her mom said. "Then I tasted the fish and started choking."

"Choking?" Marti asked.

"Yes. The fish was really dry. Your dad can't cook fish. Anyway, he gave me a glass of water." She smiled at the memory. "I knew he was the one for me."

Lizzie was confused. How was a story about choking on some fish going to help her figure out what to do about Jamie? "Let me get this straight," she said. "You're choking and you're thinking, *I really like this guy?*"

"I don't know. Somewhere in there I just suddenly knew. He was the one," Nora said.

"Grown-ups are weird," Marti said.

"Very weird," Lizzie agreed. She didn't think she'd be swallowing a dry hamburger in the school cafeteria and then—*boom!*—she'd know how she felt about Jamie. She wondered if Sarah and Olivier were still on the TV.

As she reached for the clicker, the doorbell rang. "If

that's Jamie, I'm not here," she warned her mother. Then she sprinted to the safety of her room.

Since Mom has the whole boy thing worked out already, Lizzie decided, *I'll let her figure out what to do about Jamie!*

CHAPTER SEVEN

When she came home, Casey was surprised to see
Jamie at the front door.

Her mom stood in the entryway. "Hi, Jamie. Ah . . .
Lizzie can't come to the door right now."

"Why?" Jamie asked, shoving his hands deep into the
pockets of his fleece jacket.

Her mom bit her lip, clearly uncomfortable. "Uh . . .
I'm not really sure."

"Oh, well, can I come in and wait until you find out?"
Jamie asked.

"Okay." Her mom gave Casey a "help me" look. Casey
felt bad. Her mom was clueless about the whole Liz-Jamie-
Rod love triangle.

"Hi, Jamie," Casey said, walking in behind him.
"Where's Liz?"

"She might be upstairs," her mother offered.

"I'll go check," Casey said.

Her mother looked relieved. "I'll go start dinner." Quickly, she disappeared into the kitchen.

"Do you want to watch cartoons?" Marti asked Jamie.

Jamie's eyes followed Casey heading up the stairs. "Sure," he said. He settled next to Marti on the sofa.

Casey pushed opened the door to Lizzie's room. Wow! Her sister's room was a mess. Inside-out clothes blanketed the peach rug. Balls of crumpled notebook paper littered the area around the wastebasket. Lizzie's aim obviously wasn't so great. Stuffed animals, foam soccer balls, and video game cartridges covered her desk. Lizzie was nowhere to be found. Casey hoped she hadn't barricaded herself in *Casey's* room.

She backed out, then stopped abruptly. The lumpy comforter on the unmade bed wriggled and squirmed. *Sheets don't move by themselves,* Casey realized. She pulled back the blankets. "Gotcha!"

Lizzie grimaced and dove under the covers again. She held them tightly over her face.

"Liz, Jamie's downstairs and I don't think he's leaving until he talks to you."

"Sure, he will." Lizzie's voice was muffled. "His curfew is six-thirty."

"Look, Liz, I know this is really awkward, but you've got to tell Jamie now that you don't feel the way he does," Casey said. "It's too cruel to wait any longer."

"I can't do that here. Marti will be spying on me. Edwin will be coaching me. Mom will be listening so she can call Jamie's mom and discuss the whole thing. It's too public!" she wailed.

Casey placed her hand on Lizzie's knee. Or maybe it was an elbow. It was hard to tell. She was about to spin some words of sisterly wisdom—what exactly she wasn't sure—when the doorbell rang.

"Casey! Casey!" Marti screamed. "Max is here!"

"Ugh! Someone else to witness my humiliation," Lizzie groaned.

"Hold that thought," Casey said. "I'll be right back." She hurried down the stairs.

"Max, what are you doing here?" she asked.

"I thought I'd surprise you." He grinned, looking pleased with his thoughtfulness. "I haven't seen you much lately." He laced his fingers through hers.

"It's a nice surprise." Casey liked the warmth of his palm against hers.

"What's up?" Max asked. "You've been barely texting. And I know you love to text."

"True. Just busy with other things." Casey tried to be vague, but it was hard. She wanted to share everything with him. But she cautioned herself not to bore him with details.

"Hey, Casey!" Jamie called from the sofa. "Is Lizzie coming down soon?"

"I'm on it," Casey promised.

"Why don't we go hang somewhere? We could take a drive?" Max suggested.

"I need to talk to Lizzie," Casey said.

"Your little sister? Can't it wait?" He pulled her gently toward him.

Casey glanced back at Jamie. She could see the sadness in his eyes. "No, it can't. But I'll be fast," she promised. She led Max over to the sofa. "This is Jamie. Watch cartoons with him and Marti till I get back."

"Are you serious?" Max seemed shocked.

Casey pushed him down between her six-year-old stepsister and the ten-year-old boy who liked her sister but whom her sister didn't like back. "It'll be fun!"

• • • • •

"This stinks!" Derek kicked the rock and watched it bounce along the sidewalk.

"Totally, man. How could you leave me high and dry like that?" Sam asked, slinging his camouflage backpack over his left shoulder.

"Oh, yeah, like I really planned for my car to get a flat tire," Derek grumbled. Sam had been with Derek this morning when he'd run over the rusty nail. The tire went *phfut*! Derek knew it was an easy patch and the tire would be fine. Nora was actually being a sport and getting it fixed for him. But for now, they were hoofing it home from school.

"This walk is totally wearing out the treads of my new kicks." Derek looked down at his retro blue and white sneakers. If he'd known he'd be hiking home, he never would have worn them.

"Wanna shoot some hoops later?" Sam asked, purposely knocking some dead leaves onto Derek's sneakers.

"Lay off!" Derek knocked the leaves back. "I gotta work."

Sam smirked. "Oh, yeah, cute waitress."

"Yeah, cute waitress," Derek repeated. He still couldn't get Sally out of his mind. And that bothered him. He never got hung up on a girl. Girls got hung up on *him*.

"Making your move tonight? Asking her out, huh?" Sam nodded as if it were a given. And with Derek, it should've been. He never hesitated to ask out a girl. But this time, for the first time, he was nervous.

The boyfriend's gone, he told himself. *She'll jump at the chance to be with me.*

Then he had an awful thought. What if she'd gotten back together with the boyfriend? Girls were weird like that—saying they hate a guy one day and then the next, they're back with the dude, all lovey-dovey.

"I gotta make sure the boyfriend is truly out," Derek told Sam. He pulled his cell from his pocket.

"You're going to call and ask her that?" Sam sounded incredulous.

"No," Derek said, dialing her number, which he had swiped from the Smelly Nelly's manager's notebook. "Watch and learn."

Sally picked up on the second ring. Derek pretended that he forgot the work schedule.

"You're on tonight," Sally said. "With me."

"So do you need a ride?" Derek hoped Nora had gotten his tire fixed. Otherwise, he would have to do it—pronto.

"No, I'm good. My mom's dropping me off."

"No boyfriend-chauffeur service?" Derek asked casually.

"Of course not," Sally replied as if this were old news.

"So you're really flying solo, huh?" Derek joked. But it wasn't a joke. He needed confirmation.

"All by myself," Sally agreed. She hesitated. "Are you all right?"

"Totally cool. Later!" He snapped the phone shut and grinned. He raised his hand and high-fived Sam.

"All systems go?" Sam asked before he turned onto the street that led to his own house.

"You know it. Dating Derek is back!" Derek could already imagine what an awesome couple he and Sally would make. "Tonight I turn on the charm."

Sam shook his head in amazement. "I don't know how you get all the girls, man. You make it look so easy."

Derek shrugged. "What can I say? I have a gift . . . a talent . . . maybe, even, a skill. Girls can't help but want to be near me." He jogged toward his house. He needed to check on his car. There was no way he was getting to work late tonight!

Derek burst through the front door, beaming. The car was in the driveway—the tire patched, pumped, and ready to hit the pavement. *Nora is great. Tonight I'm going to take out the garbage without being asked,* he vowed. *Hey, I may even clean my room!*

He stopped short in front of the living room sofa. "Jamie! Max! You guys come over to watch cartoons? By yourselves?" He laughed.

"Not exactly," Jamie said.

"They're watching with *me*," Marti said.

"Whatever." He headed toward the kitchen to make a sandwich.

"Derek, can I ask you a question?" Jamie asked hesitantly.

"Ask away," Derek said, still in a good mood. He stopped by the sofa.

"Have you ever liked a girl, but she didn't like you that way?"

Derek searched his memory. "No . . . not really."

"Well, I told your stepsister I liked her, and now she's acting really strangely," Jamie said.

"Casey? She was born strange!" Derek quipped.

"Hey!" Max protested.

"Oh, yeah, sorry," Derek said. "But she is a *little* strange, right?"

Max scowled. "Only lately . . ."

"No, the other sister," Jamie interrupted. "Lizzie."

"Oh. Good choice." Derek wasn't sure what he was supposed to say.

"So how do I get her to like me?" Jamie asked.

Ugh. Derek hated all this relationship advice stuff. He turned to Max. "Any ideas for the kid?"

"You should compliment her," Max suggested.

"Really?" Jamie seemed interested. "Like how?"

"You know, say her hair looks nice. Or her outfit is cool. Girls like that stuff," Max answered.

"And don't gross her out," Derek added. "Girls don't dig bodily noises." He belched for effect.

"And try to touch her," Max said.

"*Touch* her?" Jamie gasped, horrified.

"Yeah. Give her a high five," Max suggested. "Or ask to borrow a pencil and then touch her hand when you reach for it. Gotta make contact."

Derek leaned over the sofa and sniffed at Jamie.

"Get back! What're you doing?" Jamie cried.

"Just checking," Derek said. "You gotta smell good. Girls like guys who smell good. I'm thinking you need a shower."

Marti leaned over to Jamie and took a dramatic sniff. "I agree. You need a bath."

Jamie's face turned red. "Gimme a break. I just played soccer." He sighed. "This girl stuff is tricky."

• • • • •

Meanwhile, Casey made herself comfortable on the end of Lizzie's bed. Lizzie slowly peeked out from the safety of her blankets.

"I have an idea," Casey announced.

"Banish Jamie from our house forever?" Lizzie asked hopefully.

Casey yanked one of Lizzie's braids. "No, silly. You two need to talk, but somewhere more public than here. It won't be so weird if there are other people around. You could go to the park . . . or Smelly Nelly's."

Lizzie shook her head. "That's still too private."

Casey racked her brain for another solution. Max was waiting for her. Jamie was waiting for Lizzie. She had to move things forward. "Okay, um . . . well . . . if you want, I could come with you—unless you think that would be weird."

Lizzie beamed. "No, that's not weird! That's good! You can be my coach!" She grabbed both of Casey's hands. "And promise that you won't leave us alone."

"Mm-hmm." Casey smiled.

"Even better," Lizzie said. "We could all go to Smelly Nelly's together, and you could tell him how I feel, and I could listen and nod!"

"Not a chance!" Casey grabbed the covers and pulled them back over her sister's head.

"It's gonna be a disaster!" Lizzie cried from underneath.

"It's going to be great," Casey promised as she stood. "Get yourself together," she commanded. "We're going out."

Casey hurried across the hall to her own room. She had a new idea. She was going to make the conversation with Jamie a whole lot easier for Lizzie. Closing her door, Casey felt like a secret agent. A secret *love* agent.

Flicking open her cell phone, she dialed 411. The operator connected her to Rod's house.

After an embarrassing exchange where Casey had to ask his bewildered mother to speak with him, Casey finally got Rod on the phone. She introduced herself as the reporter from the pool, then she mentioned that she also happened to be Lizzie's older sister. Oddly enough, Rod wasn't freaked out.

She invited him to Smelly Nelly's—to go on a date with her sister. She promised Rod that Lizzie was *really* into him.

He was all for it. *Perfect!*

Casey hurried down the stairs. The plan was in motion.

Jamie sat between Max and Derek on the sofa. All

three guys were eating huge sandwiches piled with turkey, salami, cheese, and who knows what else they found in the kitchen. Wrestling was on the TV. Marti had left to play with her stuffed animals in her room.

"Hey, Jamie," Casey called. "Lizzie was wondering if you'd like to come to Smelly Nelly's with us after dinner."

"You, me, and Lizzie?" Jamie asked.

"Yeah."

"That sounds . . . weird," Jamie said.

Derek chewed a huge bite. "Yeah. It really does."

Casey swatted Derek on the head. She turned back to Jamie. "You'll come, right?"

Jamie looked unsure. He turned to Derek. "Are you gonna be there?" he asked. "'Cause I might need a pep talk."

Derek rolled his eyes. "Yeah, I'll be there. I work there. But, Casey, don't sit in my section. I know how bad you tip!"

All of a sudden, Jamie sniffed the crease of his elbow. He made a disgusted face and bolted off the sofa. "I gotta go home. See you later. Bye, guys." He hurried toward the front door. "Bye, Lizzie," he called up the stairs.

"Boys are strange," Casey said as she watched him

leave. She squeezed onto the sofa between Max and Derek. "Derek, isn't it so cute how Jamie looks up to you?"

"Adorable," Derek remarked. "Can I go now?"

Casey held him by his arm. "Look, Derek, you've gotta be extra careful when dealing with kids this age," she warned. "This is a very tricky situation. Lizzie is traumatized, and Jamie could be scarred for life."

"Got it!" Derek tried to stand, but Casey pulled him back down.

"Don't you want to know why?" she asked.

"No." Derek finished the last of his sandwich.

"Because Lizzie doesn't like Jamie. She likes Rod! Isn't this awful?" she cried.

Derek shook her off. "Casey, I don't do this. Okay? See ya!" He took the steps two at a time and made for his room.

"So you ready to go out now?" Max asked.

Casey turned to her boyfriend. He was so calm, so patient, sitting through all this drama. She felt bad. She couldn't put him through any more of this. Too much more family drama and he'd be sure to bolt.

"You should go home," she said. "Today's kind of crazy."

"But I've been sitting here—"

"I know," Casey said, pulling him off the sofa and leading him to the door. "I appreciate that. But I have all this stuff going on with Lizzie."

"Yeah, sounds heavy. I can come along, if you want—"

"No, no. You don't want to do that. Go home. Play some video games," Casey suggested.

"I don't want to play video games," Max said, his voice tight.

"Well, then call your friends. Hang with them," Casey said. She smiled while she talked, but it was difficult. She didn't want to give Max his space. She wanted him to be with her. Now. Always.

"I'm sick of hanging with them!" Max exclaimed. "And I'm sick of all this!" Max stormed out the door, slamming it with such force, the vase on the side table shook.

Casey stood, stunned. She had never seen Max lose his temper before. What had happened?

She was being the perfect girlfriend.

So why was her boyfriend so angry?

CHAPTER EIGHT

"Whoa! What's up? Your parents finally kick you out of the house?" Carlos asked as he spread a thin layer of peanut butter on twelve-grain bread.

"No. Why?" Derek hung his coat on one of the pegs in the kitchen. He grabbed his order pad and a pen and poked his finger into the jar of organic peanut butter.

"You're here early," Carlos said, pulling the jar away from Derek.

"What can I say? I'm good at my job!" Derek licked his finger. Not bad! He headed out to the front of the restaurant. He wanted to look busy when Sally arrived.

And busy he was. Smelly Nelly's soon filled up with kids from the lacrosse team downing donuts, ladies in a book club asking for herbal tea, and three families begging for refills on the sweet potato fries. Derek saw

Sally, but kept missing the chance to talk to her. One of them was always running to pick up an order or clear a table.

"Hey, how you doin'?" Derek finally asked. He waited by the counter as she topped a mug of hot chocolate with whipped cream.

"I'm fine. How are you?" Sally made a fluffy, white swirl atop the steaming drink.

"Oh, you know. It's all good." Derek pretended to be really focused on pouring a chai latte. "So, you talk to your boyfriend again?"

"Oh, yeah. All taken care of," Sally said, sprinkling chocolate shavings on the whipped cream.

"Really?" Derek tried to control his voice. Not sound too excited. "You don't seem very upset."

"No. Why would I be?"

"No reason at all." Derek took a deep breath. "So, I was wondering if you and I—"

"Miss! Miss!" called a balding man at table seven.

"He wants his cocoa. Bad," Sally said. She headed off to deliver the hot chocolate. Derek's eyes trailed her. *Later*, he thought.

Then he groaned. Casey, Lizzie, and a bewildered Jamie slid into a booth in his section. "Here's trouble," he greeted them. "What can I get you guys?" he asked in his most official waiter voice.

Casey's eyes twinkled. "Hmmmm. Derek waiting on me? You know, I could get used to this."

"Yeah, well don't," Derek taunted. "I'm only serving the kids."

"Fine," Casey huffed. "I'll guess I'll have to move to a different table."

"No!" cried Lizzie.

"Okay," Jamie said at the same time.

Casey stood and slid into the booth behind theirs.

"Look, I got other tables. What do you want?" Derek asked. His gaze kept straying to Sally. She had her hair up in a high ponytail today, and she wore big gold hoop earrings.

"I'll have a chocolate shake," Jamie said.

"Yeah, me too, and if you can bring me a sister who isn't a liar,"—Lizzie glared daggers at Casey—"that would be great!"

Derek snickered. "No Casey. Coming right up."

He hurried to bring the order to the kitchen. He usually never moved this fast, but Sally was tracking toward the kitchen, too.

"Busy, huh?" Derek said as he accidentally-on-purpose bumped into her.

"Completely." Sally ripped an order off her pad and handed it to Carlos.

"So, any big weekend plans?" Derek asked.

"Nothing major." Sally smiled as she dumped a handful of veggie chips on the side of a plate.

A smile. *A smile means she's interested.* "I was thinking of going to see the new Will Smith movie. You know, the one where he battles the Ice Age Cro-Magnon man."

"Seriously?" Sally wrinkled her nose. "The zombie horror flick where they stalk the crazed vampires looks much better."

Derek almost fell over. This girl liked zombies and crazed vampires! "So . . . uh . . . how about we go—"

"Order's up!" Carlos yelled, even though he was standing inches away. "Derek, you got an order for me or you think I'm performing dinner theater back here?"

Derek watched Sally carry her food out to her customer. He ripped the paper off his pad and flung it at Carlos. "Here."

Why is asking her out so hard? he wondered. He was angry at himself. He was making a big deal of this. He was caring way too much.

• • • • •

"Max? Max, please call me back. I really want to talk to you." Casey left her fourteenth message since he had stormed away this afternoon. Why wasn't he picking up? Why wasn't he calling back?

Casey scanned her text messages. Nothing since she checked ten seconds ago.

She was confused. She and Max just had their first big fight and she had no idea why. She just couldn't figure it out.

"Casey. Casey!" Lizzie whispered from the booth behind her.

Casey leaned toward her sister. "Do something!" Lizzie hissed.

Lizzie and Jamie sat across from each other, each intently sipping a chocolate milkshake. Neither spoke. No eye contact. Nothing. Just *slurp, slurp.*

"Liz, just talk to him!" she whispered back.

"Nice weather, huh?" Lizzie mumbled to Jamie. Casey groaned. Did she have to do everything?

"Your hair looks good," Jamie blurted out.

Lizzie pulled the two braids out from either side of her head, inspected them quickly, and let them flop down onto her neck. "What are you talking about?" she demanded.

"The braids . . . they, uh, are . . . very braided. Kind of like one of those braided breads in the bakery. Only better, I mean. Uh . . . better braiding," Jamie rambled nervously. He reached out, as if to touch Lizzie's arm, but quickly pulled back.

Casey was torn. She really wanted to track down Max. She thought of calling him at Clink's house. But, one look at Lizzie and Jamie told her that their time bomb was ticking—*fast.*

Where is Rod? she wondered. She couldn't rely on an eleven-year-old—that was for sure. Reinforcements were needed. Casey surveyed the restaurant for help. The old bald guy with his family wouldn't cut it. And the lacrosse team was already heading out the door. She cringed. She had only one choice.

"Jamie, come with me," Casey instructed. She motioned Jamie over to the counter, where Derek stood.

"Jamie needs help," Casey announced.

"The bathroom's around the corner," Derek said, distracted. Casey followed his eyes, zeroing in on the cute waitress. *Figures!*

"Derek, what should I do? The compliment thing didn't work. And Lizzie won't even look at me," Jamie complained.

97

At that moment, the cute tanned waitress walked by, weighed down by a tray piled with dirty dishes.

"Let me help," Derek offered.

Casey stared, her mouth agape, as normally selfish Derek reached for the tray and brought it into the kitchen.

"Thanks," the waitress said, moving onto her next table.

"You like her," Casey accused when Derek returned.

"No way!" Derek cried. "Okay, maybe."

"I thought you weren't being dragged into any more relationships," Casey said, arching her eyebrows.

"This won't be a *relationship*. Sally's very straightforward. No game playing for her," Derek boasted.

"If you've got it all figured out, then why haven't you asked her out yet?"

"I'm working on it," Derek admitted. "Not that it's any of your business. Where's your boyfriend?"

Casey blushed. Derek always knew which buttons to press to annoy her. It was embarrassing not to know where Max was. Even more infuriating not to know why he was so angry.

"Hey, what about me?" Jamie piped up.

"Look, Jamie. I understand why you like Liz, because, unlike her sister, she's pretty cool," Derek began.

"Ha, ha," Casey muttered.

"But, Jamie," Derek continued, placing his hand on the younger boy's shoulder, "if she likes another guy, you just gotta chillz."

Jamie's face drained of color. "Lizzie likes another guy?"

"Good going!" Casey swatted Derek.

Derek stared at Jamie. "You don't know about Rod?"

"Lizzie likes *Rod*?" he cried.

Derek shut his eyes and shook his head. "See," he said to Casey, "this is why I don't get involved in this stuff."

"I can't believe it," Jamie mumbled.

"You *need* to fix this," Casey instructed Derek. "Help him."

Derek poured Jamie a lemonade and slid it across the counter to him. "Jamie, you gotta take it like a man. Life is harsh. The polar ice caps are melting. Manatees are dying. And girls just make your life miserable." Derek popped a straw in the drink. "My advice: Close off your heart. Face reality, but don't get involved."

Jamie nodded seriously, slurping his lemonade.

Casey laid her head in her hands and groaned. "That's not what I meant when I said *fix this*!"

CHAPTER NINE

Dear Diary,

What the Grinch is to Christmas, Derek is to love. How can he truly have no feelings? Maybe his heart is two times too small!

He was so harsh to poor Jamie. Sure, he needed to find out that Lizzie's heart beats for another, but that's not how the discovery was supposed to be made. I had it all planned out: Rod swoops into Smelly Nelly's. Their eyes meet and Rod gathers Lizzie in his arms. Their connection is so powerful, so blinding, that Jamie instantly realizes that he can't stand in their way. He's happy just being Lizzie's friend. And everyone lives happily ever after—thanks to ME!

But now Derek has messed it up. **Boo hoo!**

He is blind to people, blind to their feelings. Me—I can read people. I know what people want, even before they know it themselves. It's a talent I have.

Ha! Maybe you and your crystal ball should run away and join the circus. I hear they need more clown acts!

Not funny, Derek! STOP reading my journal!

♡ Love,

Casey

• • • • •

Lizzie watched Jamie as he talked with Derek and Casey. She could only imagine what horrible things they were telling him. Swirling her straw in the melting remains of her milkshake, Lizzie knew avoiding Jamie was over. She'd dragged this out long enough. She needed to tell Jamie she wasn't going to be his girlfriend.

She tried to slurp the rest of the chocolate ice cream. She could see the brown mixture lodged in the straw. It wouldn't go up or down. She inhaled deeply, working at it. Then she gave up.

It's kind of like me and Jamie, Lizzie realized. She was stuck. She knew she should tell Jamie that she just wanted to be his friend. That's all. Nothing else. But, somehow, she just couldn't. Couldn't get the words out of her mouth.

Jamie slid back into the booth, across from her. Lizzie could read his body language—the way he slumped, the way he furrowed his brows. He didn't look so eager anymore. He looked, well, angry.

"Jamie, we need to talk," she said.

"Finally." Jamie stared at her.

"'Cause I'm sure Casey won't let me leave the restaurant if I don't!" Lizzie tried to make a joke. Jamie liked jokes. But now he wasn't laughing.

"It's for your own good!" Casey called from the counter.

Did Casey have supersonic hearing?

"It's just, I guess I was surprised you said what you said," Lizzie started to tell Jamie.

"Look, just forget it. I'm totally over it now. I mean, over you," Jamie replied. "I like Helen."

"Helen?" Lizzie wasn't sure she heard right.

"Yeah, she's cool, don't you think?" Jamie asked.

Lizzie was speechless. He knew she thought Helen was an airhead. Jamie—at least, the Jamie who'd been her best friend—used to make fun of Helen with her. And now he *liked* her?

Lizzie felt as if the restaurant was spinning. She couldn't think. What was wrong with her? *This is good,* she told herself. *He likes someone else. I'm off the hook.*

But it wasn't good. It made her feel unbalanced, like

someone was rocking the booth. Hard. Cool? Helen?

"Not really," she mumbled. She couldn't look at him.

"Oh, well, I'm thinking of asking Helen to go with me to that new fantasy movie. You know, the one with the dragons that travel through time," Jamie said.

Lizzie knew one thing for sure, she didn't want Jamie going to a movie with Helen. *She* wanted to go to the movie with him. They always went to fantasy movies together. It was as if she'd been slapped in the face.

I'm jealous, she realized.

But why? Why should she care if he wanted to hang out with Helen?

Then it hit her—like a soccer ball to the head. *I like Jamie,* she suddenly realized. *I* like *like Jamie.*

She rapidly twirled her straw around the tall glass. She had liked him all along, she understood now. But these feelings were so new, so hard to understand. It was scary. She didn't know what to do next. She didn't know what to say. *Should I tell him?* she worried.

"Hey there, Lizzie!"

She whirled around, startled by the interruption. Rod! *Why is Rod Morrow in Smelly Nelly's? And why is he talking to me?*

"Hi, Rod," she said hesitantly.

"Scoot over, okay," Rod said. He slid next to her on the vinyl bench. "How's it going, Jamie?"

"Fine," Jamie said tightly, refusing to look at Rod.

Out of nowhere, Rod placed his clammy hand on top of hers. Lizzie stared down, frozen. Her brain couldn't compute this fast. Why was Rod holding her hand? She pulled back. "What are you doing?" she demanded. "Why are you here?"

"Lizzie, it's okay," Jamie said, before Rod could answer. "I already know you like Rod."

Rod beamed, swiping his long black hair out of his eyes.

"What?" Lizzie was bewildered. "Did Casey tell you that?"

"No, Derek," Jamie said. "But it's chillz."

"It's not chillz!" Lizzie practically shouted. She turned to Rod. "Who told you to come here?"

She knew the answer before he said it.

"Casey."

She took a deep breath. She glanced at Rod, who gave her a dopey, adoring gaze. She glanced at Jamie, who looked as if his puppy had died.

Standing up, Lizzie yelled, "Casey!" She didn't care that everyone in the café was staring at her. This was an emergency.

Casey couldn't believe that her sister had just screeched her name so loudly. What was wrong?

Lizzie hurried over, grabbed the sleeve of Casey's pink sweater, and pulled her into a corner. "What did you do?" Lizzie demanded.

"Nothing," Casey said.

"Why is Rod here?" Lizzie asked. "What did you tell him?"

"Me? Why do you think I had anything to do with it?" Casey asked. She wanted Lizzie to believe that Rod came here on his own, that he liked her that much.

"He told me it was you. Spill it," Lizzie commanded.

Casey had no choice. She told the whole, embarrassing truth.

"How could you?" Lizzie cried. All the color had drained from her face. Her freckles popped out vividly against her now-pale skin. "I don't like Rod."

"You don't?" Now it was Casey's turn to be confused.

"No, I just told you that to get you off my back," Lizzie said.

"But, why would you do that?"

"Because you wouldn't stop. You kept getting involved. You kept wanting me to have a boyfriend!" Lizzie cried. Then she admitted softly, "And, maybe, I'm not ready for a boyfriend. But, maybe . . . maybe I was too embarrassed to tell you that."

Casey couldn't believe how blind she'd been. She felt horrible. "So you told me you liked Rod, so I'd stop asking you about Jamie?"

Lizzie nodded and bit her lip. "Yeah. I just said Rod because all the girls at school think he's cute. I don't. He's kind of an idiot."

Casey nodded and smiled. "Kind of." She hugged her sister. "I'm so sorry. I should have minded my own business."

"True," Lizzie agreed. She glanced back at the booth. Jamie and Rod both seemed to be inspecting the ceiling. "You need to get rid of Rod."

"Me?" squealed Casey.

"Yeah. You got him here. You get him outta here," Lizzie said.

"How?" It was a lot easier to get into a mess like this than to get out. But Casey owed Lizzie.

"You're the one with all the brilliant ideas. Write another article," Lizzie suggested.

Casey smiled. As always, another great plan had come to her. "I've got a better idea." She hurried into the kitchen and found Derek.

"I need you to do me a small favor." It wasn't easy asking Derek for favors.

"Not likely," Derek said.

"Is there a camera here?" she asked.

"Like I know." Derek rolled his eyes.

"In the drawer under the counter!" Carlos yelled.

"Thanks. Derek, all I need you to do is help me get rid of Rod. Turns out Lizzie doesn't like him," Casey explained.

"I told you not to get involved. No, in fact, I warned you. When will you realize that I am oh-so-much wiser than you are?" Derek gave her a superior grin.

"Never," Casey said. "Are you going to help me or not?"

"Not," said Derek.

Ugh! He could be so infuriating! *I don't need Derek*, she decided. She had another way to pull off her plan. She ran to the counter, found the small digital camera, and returned to the tables. A moment later, she emerged— without Derek.

Casey walked over to the boys' table. Lizzie followed.

"Hi, Rod!" Casey said. "Glad you could make it."

"Hey," Rod said uncomfortably. "I think you might've been wrong with your info. About Lizzie."

Casey nodded. "You know us girls. Like a guy one minute and then, not so much the next." She shrugged, as if it happened all the time. "But I've got a surprise for you."

"Really?" Rod asked.

"Really?" Lizzie echoed.

"Yep. My photographer is in the kitchen. He wants to take your picture right now!" Casey exclaimed.

"He's in the kitchen?" Rod seemed skeptical.

"Hey, the man has to make money somehow. Sports photography doesn't pay much. You ready?" Casey asked Rod.

"Now? But I would've washed my hair or something," Rod said.

Casey grabbed his hand. "Carlos has his camera now. Come on, you look great."

Rod followed Casey toward the kitchen. "Can we take a lot of different shots, you know, to be sure?"

"Absolutely," Casey agreed.

"When's this going to be in the paper?" Rod asked.

"I'm working on it," Casey said. She made a mental note to ask —no, beg—the high school newspaper to print the article. Not that she'd written anything. Yet.

She took a quick glance at her phone. No messages.

Well, she realized with a painful ache of regret, *if Max is still angry, I'll have a lot of time to write articles about eleven-year-old swimmers.*

CHAPTER TEN

"That was weird," Lizzie said, sliding back into her seat, as Rod trailed after Casey.

"Yeah." Jamie was doing that twiddling fingers thing again.

"Listen, I never wanted to hang out with Rod. I didn't ask him here," Lizzie explained.

"Then why'd he show up?" Jamie asked.

"Casey." Lizzie liked that Jamie nodded. He got it. He'd spent enough time at her house to understand her family.

"So," Lizzie tried her best to sound disinterested, "when did you start liking Helen?"

Jamie blushed. "Since Derek told me you started liking Rod."

"So you don't like her?" Lizzie asked. She wanted to be sure about this.

"Nope. And you don't like him?"

"Nope," Lizzie said.

They sat in silence for a few minutes. She pressed her fingernails into the palm of her hand. She knew they'd leave marks on her skin.

I'll do it, she decided. *I'll do it really fast—just like jumping into a freezing pool. It's probably worse if I think about it too much.*

"Look, maybe I could get used to the idea of you liking me," Lizzie told Jamie. She turned her gaze away from him, focusing on the shiny tabletop. "And maybe . . . me liking you."

"Really?" Jamie sounded surprised.

Lizzie snuck a quick glance at his face. He was grinning.

"There are rules," Lizzie announced, finally meeting his eyes. She didn't want him getting any wrong ideas. "I'm not going to act like Helen and Sophia. I'm not going to start wearing pink and flipping my hair and giggling all the time—"

"I don't want you to," Jamie interrupted.

"Good. I'm just going to be me. And you have to be you. And we still have to be best friends and play video games and soccer. And, maybe if you give me some time—

like I said—well, maybe, you and I . . ." Lizzie felt herself blabbering. She clamped her mouth shut.

"Great," he said, beaming. "Fine. I mean, take your time."

Lizzie smiled, too. She was glad she'd told him. Maybe everything would be okay between them.

"So . . . do you like me yet?" Jamie asked.

Lizzie laughed. "Don't push it," she warned.

Jamie laughed, too. "How about now?" he teased.

"How about we make Derek get us some cookies?" Lizzie suggested.

"You're on!" Jamie said. He reached across the table. *Up, down, slap, slap, snap.* Their victory handshake.

Lizzie smiled. Her best friend was back. And, as far as she could tell, there was nothing wrong with having a best friend you *liked* liked. It actually might be kind of cool.

• • • • •

Derek hung around in the kitchen as much as he could. It was a good, private place to try to talk to Sally. Except the girl was in constant motion. In to pick up an order. Rushing out to deliver the food. Hurrying in to drop off an order. Derek could never find a moment alone with her.

By the end of the night, Smelly Nelly's had almost cleared out. Rod was long gone. Lizzie and Jamie were sharing cookies and playing paper football with a folded napkin. Casey still sat at the counter, sipping hot chocolate and mentally psyching her phone to ring. But most everyone else had left.

Sally entered the kitchen, finally with nothing to do but clean up.

"Ahem, Carlos?" Derek nodded toward the back door. This was the signal they had agreed upon.

"Oh, yeah, I have to make a phone call," Carlos said loudly. "Outside!" He rushed out the back door, winking at Derek as he left. Not too obvious!

"So your stepsisters are here." Sally straightened a stack of menus. "You should introduce me."

"Not necessary," Derek said, waving off the idea with his hand. "Besides, they're all caught up in a little kid soap opera."

"Oh." She reached for the broom and began to sweep.

"Listen, um, you know my 'no dating' rule?" Derek asked.

"Yeah." She didn't even look up.

"Well, it turns out it was more of a temporary philosophy," he continued.

Sally smiled knowingly. "Oh, right! So who is this cute customer that you've given up your philosophy for?"

"Actually, it's not a customer." He stared at her, making sure she saw that extra twinkle in his eye.

"Then who is it?" Sally grinned.

Derek grinned back. *She knows it's her, and she's playing along. She likes me. Excellent!* He could sense the connection between them.

"It's—"

"Patrick!" Sally cried.

"Patrick? Who's Patrick?" Derek whirled around and gaped at the blond-haired guy who had just come through the back door. Then it hit him. Patrick was her ex-boyfriend.

"What are you doing here?" Sally demanded.

Good question! Derek thought. He could tell she was annoyed. He was annoyed, too.

Patrick raised his arms in surrender. "I thought I would surprise you. You know, make up for being such a jerk and everything. So let's go out." He reached for Sally's arm. "I'm taking you out."

Sally pushed him away and leaned on the broom handle. "No, I can't do this now, Patrick."

Derek watched Sally closely. She wasn't happy that

Patrick was here. *The stupid guy doesn't know he's outta the picture,* he thought.

"Why not?" Patrick demanded. He stepped toward her. Reached for her.

Derek leaped in front of him. He grabbed Patrick's arm before he could touch Sally. "Dude, you heard the lady. She can't do this! Back off!"

Patrick shoved him away. He was a lot taller than Derek. "Whoa! Get your hands off me! Who are you?"

"I'm the one who's giving it to you straight. Take a hint! It's over between you and Sally. She's done with you."

"Derek!" Sally cried.

"Seriously, dude," Derek said, leading Patrick toward the door. "You two are finished. She told me."

"What?" Patrick was both confused and angry. "Sal, what did you tell this guy?"

"I didn't—" Sally tried to come between him and Derek.

But Derek jumped in again. "You're broken up. Finished. Finito! Sally doesn't want to see you again. She's moving on—and so should you." He opened the door.

Patrick's face turned crimson. "I knew something was up, Sally. You're with this clown, aren't you?" He pointed to Derek. "I should've known! Well, I guess you're right. It's over. I can't believe you'd be this cruel."

With that, Patrick left, dramatically slamming the door.

Derek could feel the adrenaline rush through his body. He was pumped up, energized. He had just saved the beautiful girl from her horrible ex-boyfriend. He was invincible! A hero!

He turned to Sally, ready for his thank-you hug. Maybe even a kiss.

"Are you crazy?" she screamed instead. Her face was flushed and her eyes were wide. Then she pulled her right arm back—and punched him in the stomach!

CHAPTER ELEVEN

Derek sucked in his breath. "Whoa!" Did he just get hit—*by a girl*?

He grabbed his stomach. She'd missed his ribs and, luckily, it wasn't too hard of a punch. He was okay. It was more the shock. He never saw it coming.

"You're the crazy one!" he cried. "Ever hear of Houdini? You could kill a guy by punching him in the stomach."

"Oh, please. You're such a drama queen. You deserved it." Sally glared at him. She didn't ask if he was hurt.

"Okay, you've lost me," Derek said. He took a step back. He wanted a little distance between her and her fists. "Why'd you do that?"

"Because you just ruined everything!" she shouted. "What gives you the right to break up with my boyfriend for me?"

"Are you blind? I was helping you. Your ex wanted you

back. He was going to get all violent or something if I hadn't saved you." Derek was still waiting for his thank you. He was beginning to suspect it wasn't coming.

"Get over yourself, Derek Venturi! First, I don't need saving," Sally said. "And second, Patrick's not my ex. He's my boyfriend. I never broke up with him."

"But you said it was over," Derek answered.

"I did not." Sally shook her head in disbelief. "You only heard what you wanted to hear. I just said the conversation was over."

"But you just told him you couldn't do this now," Derek said.

"When I said I couldn't do this now, what I meant was I had to clean up *before* I left," Sally explained. "And now you have Patrick all angry and upset, thinking we're broken up!"

"Do you want to break up with him?" Derek asked hopefully.

"No! I like Patrick. We're good together. Or we were until you came along," Sally ranted. "You know, I don't get you. You walk around boasting that you 'don't do relationships, don't talk relationships.' So what are you doing messing with *my* relationship?"

Derek shrugged. He had no idea how this had spiraled

so out of control. No. He did know. He let himself have feelings for Sally, and those feeling made him act crazy. He went against everything he thought he believed in. "I was just spreading the gospel of Derek. Preaching the wisdom of being single. Converting you. And Patrick." Derek tried to turn it into a joke. Add a little humor.

Sally wasn't laughing. But she didn't look as mad. And now that her anger was fading, she looked miserable. "I thought you were a decent guy. I talked to you like a friend, trusted you. I should've listened to Beth. I should've believed it when she told me that Derek only cares about Derek. That you're cold and heartless." Sally grabbed the dustbin and headed into the café, still carrying the broom.

"Where are you going?" Derek asked.

"I'm going to clean up the mess out there. Then I've got to figure out a way to clean up the mess you've made for me."

Derek watched her go. He had an ache in his chest that didn't come from her punch. He felt bad, truly bad. And he wasn't thinking only about himself, about how Sally had a boyfriend and didn't want to date him. He could deal with that. He was thinking about Sally. Sally was cool . . . amazing. She shouldn't feel pain because of him.

Carlos sauntered into the kitchen. "All good?" he asked with a mischievous grin.

"Awesome!" Derek replied out of habit, giving Carlos a thumbs-up. He knew that's what Carlos expected from him. That's what everyone expected of him. The guy who always got the girl. Cool and detached.

But he wasn't. He was guilty and *involved*.

• • • • •

"How do you live with him?" the new waitress asked. She rested one hand on the counter and the other on her broom. Her name tag read SALLY.

"It's not easy," Casey admitted. "We in the McDonald-Venturi household are an elite group. Kind of like the Navy Seals of suburbia. It requires much skill and cunning to make it through life with Derek."

"I feel like squishing him with my shoe," Sally said.

"Get in line," Casey quipped.

"I—" Sally stopped when she heard the front door jingle as it opened. "Hey, we're closing."

Casey turned. "Max!" she cried. "It's okay. I know him," she told Sally.

She wanted to leap off her stool. Race from the counter and wrap her arms around him. Just the sight of him made her feel buoyant, as if she were holding onto hundreds of helium balloons and about to lift off. She didn't trust her feet on the floor, didn't trust that she wouldn't float right over to him.

She held back. She didn't want to seem too clingy—especially in front of Sally, Lizzie, and Jamie.

She walked over to him, quickly, a bounce in her step. "Max! I'm so glad you're here."

"Really?" he asked skeptically. "It's kind of hard to tell."

"Of course I am." She laced her hand through his and led him over to a table in the corner. "But we need to talk." She wasn't sure what had happened between them, but she wanted to set things right.

"Look, I know what you want to say."

"You do?" Casey had no idea what she wanted to say.

"Yeah. You want to break up with me." Max scowled.

"What?" The words came out like a whisper, although in her head she seemed to be screaming.

"It's not working out," he said. "You've made that clear all week."

Casey stared at him, not understanding. What wasn't working out? They were great together. He made her smile. They could talk to each other, have a good time together. So why didn't he want to be her boyfriend anymore?

She glanced over at Lizzie and Jamie. Had she been so involved in her little sister's love life that she'd missed what was happening in hers? A sinking feeling settled in her stomach. "Do you like someone else?"

"No!" Max seemed outraged at the suggestion. "But— but I can tell you don't like me anymore, so . . ."

"Are you kidding?" Casey reached for his hands across the table. "I totally like you. I've never stopped."

"That's not how it's felt lately," Max admitted. "You never want to be around me. You're always pushing me off on my friends. You used to always ask me questions about everything—football, my family, the TV shows I watched. But now you just don't care." He raised his voice and Casey could see Sally, who was angrily sweeping the floor, glance in their direction. "And then when you pushed me away before—well, I blew up."

"No, no, Max, that's not how it is. I mean, it's not what I meant it to be," Casey fumbled for an explanation. She took a deep breath and told him her whole 'perfect girlfriend' plan. When she finished, Max stared at her so intently, he didn't even blink. Casey couldn't imagine what he was thinking.

I've messed up, she realized. *Instead of being the best girlfriend to my boyfriend, I'm now going to be the girlfriend with no boyfriend.*

Max's eyes began to crinkle. Then he burst out laughing.

Casey didn't know what to do. She laughed along, too.

"That's ridiculous, Casey!" Max finally stopped laughing long enough to speak. "I'm not Derek. I don't want a girlfriend who gives me tons of space and makes me hang with the guys all the time. If I wanted that, I never would have asked you out."

He pulled her chair right next to his. "I like you. I like that you're always asking me questions. I like that you try to like what I like. Hey, not many girls would take the time to find out what a blitz is."

Casey smiled. "True. That took a lot of research on football websites, you know."

"I *want* to spend time with you," Max said.

"Even at my house, when my family's acting a bit crazy?" Casey asked.

"Even then," Max said.

"Great!" Casey couldn't believe how wrong she'd been. She never should have listened to Derek. She knew that feelings and getting involved in people's lives was a good

123

thing. It's what made people, people. She gave Max a big hug. "I'm sorry."

Max squeezed her hand. "Want to get out of here?"

Casey glanced over at Lizzie and Jamie. "We were going to wait for Derek to get off to give us a ride. But I think he annoyed the new waitress and now he's hiding in the kitchen."

"I'll drive everyone," Max offered.

"Really?" Casey squealed. "Hey, guys, come on, my boyfriend is driving us home." She still loved the way that word sounded—boyfriend.

Lizzie hurried over. "Everything okay with you two?"

"Yeah," Casey said. "I just need to be more involved in my own life instead of yours for a while, okay?"

Lizzie put her arm through Casey's. "Okay by me." Together they followed Max and Jamie out the door.

"Hey," Casey whispered to Lizzie. "This is like a double date! Our first sister double date!"

"Not really," said Lizzie. She had that horrified look on her face again.

"Oh, please," Casey pleaded. "I love double dates. It would be so much fun."

"Not yet," Lizzie warned Casey.

Casey nodded. "But soon, right?"

Lizzie shrugged. "I thought you were getting less involved with me and more with Max."

"True." Casey grinned and caught up with Max. "Hey, you've got to tell everyone that crazy story about your mother!"

• • • • •

Derek heard Max enter the restaurant. He knew he and Casey had some sort of fight. Any other time, he would have eavesdropped just to laugh at Casey as she groveled to make things right. But now he could only think about Sally.

He still had feelings for her. Strong feelings. And not just I-want-to-date-you feelings. They were feelings of friendship. Of wanting to make her happy—with no gain for him. They were feelings that Derek had never felt for a girl.

He had no choice. He knew what he had to do.

He raced out the back door into the parking lot. He had to find Patrick. Heading toward his own car, Derek tried to think of where the guy would go. But he didn't know the first thing about Patrick. He could be *anywhere*.

Then he spotted a figure in the driver's seat of a green

Prius parked a few spots away. The guy's head rested on the steering wheel, his hands clasped around the back of his neck. Derek knew, even before peering in the window, that this was Patrick. The poor guy never made it out of the parking lot.

He rapped on the window. Patrick jumped. Derek motioned that he wanted to talk.

Patrick rolled down the window. "What?" he asked angrily.

"Hey, dude, I want to say I'm sorry," Derek started. "It's not over. Between you and Sally, I mean."

"Then why did you say it was?" Patrick demanded.

"'Cause Sally vented to me the other day and I guess I didn't get the facts straight," Derek admitted.

Patrick seemed surprised. "She vented to *you*?"

"Yeah, but it was surprisingly quick and painless."

"Really?"

"Yeah." Derek nodded. "And there's, ah, nothing between us. At all."

Patrick sized him up. He nodded, believing his story. "So why'd she act all mean before?"

Derek explained how Sally just wanted to clean up. He convinced Patrick to go back inside. He assured Patrick that Sally was totally into him.

As Patrick returned to Smelly Nelly's, Derek leaned against the hood of his car, contemplating what to do next.

"Bye, Derek!"

He glanced up as Lizzie called to him from the back seat of Max's red car. He waved.

"George is coming home tonight," Lizzie shouted from the window. "I betcha he'll bring presents from the trip."

"Save one for me," Derek called back as they drove away. He could see Casey twisted around, telling Lizzie and Jamie a long-winded story. The four of them laughed.

From where he stood, it kind of looked as if they were all on a double date.

A few minutes later, Sally and Patrick emerged, hand in hand, from the café.

"All good?" he asked Sally. Her smile revealed the answer.

"Thanks, dude," Patrick said. Derek moved aside so Patrick could slide into his car.

Sally opened the passenger door, but hesitated before she got inside. "Why did you go after Patrick for me?" she asked.

Derek shrugged. "Seemed like the right thing. Why?"

"Well, you said you don't get involved in relationships

and that you don't have a heart, but it kind of seems like you did and you do."

Derek smirked. "Sorry. It was a temporary slip. It won't happen again."

"Good. See you at work tomorrow?" Sally asked, closing the door behind her.

"Sure thing. Have fun," he called as they drove off. *Strange*, he realized. He really meant it. He wanted her to have a good time. *I guess I do have feelings*, he thought. He grimaced. It was a good thing Casey wasn't here to witness this. She'd never let him live it down.

Derek walked slowly to his car. He'd let Carlos close up tonight. He thought about calling Sam, but then remembered that he was out with Teresa. Everyone suddenly seemed to be part of a couple, and he was by himself, single. He inhaled the crisp night air and smiled. It didn't bother him. Some frozen pizza and a PlayStation game and he was good to go. He didn't need anyone else.

At least for tonight.

There would be plenty of girls to choose from tomorrow.